Lancashire
County Council

TO CATCH A FOX

A FOX

PHILIP CAINE

TO CATCH A FOX

First paperback edition printed 2016 in the United Kingdom

ISBN 978-0-9933748-1-4

Published by PHILIP CAINE
philcaine777@hotmail.com

For more copies of this book, please email:
philcaine777@hotmail.com

Editor: Gillian Ogilvie

Cover Design: www.gonzodesign.co.uk

Printed in Great Britain by:
Orbital Print www.orbitalprint.co.uk

ABOUT THE AUTHOR

Philip has over thirty five years' experience, operating projects across three continents, within the Oil & Gas Industry. He worked the pioneering years of the North Sea, for over fifteen years on Oil Rigs, Barges & Platforms, then moved to onshore projects, spending three years in North & West Africa. Seven years were spent operating in the 'Former Soviet Union' where he managed multiple projects in Kazakhstan & Russia.

The end of the Iraq War in 2003 produced a change of client that took Philip to Baghdad, where he directed the operations and project management, of multiple accommodation bases for the American Military in Baghdad and Northern Iraq.

Philip semi-retired in 2014 and began writing in February 2015, TO CATCH A FOX is the sequel to his first novel, PICNIC IN IRAQ.

http://philcaine777.wix.com/philipcaine

Also by Philip Caine

PICNIC IN IRAQ

Do not follow life's path.
Find your own way.
And leave a wide trail….

Chinese fortune cookie….

'We few, we happy few, we band of brothers.
For he to-day that sheds his blood with me, shall be my
brother; be he 'er so vile,
for this day shall gentle his condition.
And gentlemen in England now-a-bed, shall think
themselves accursed, they were not here.
And hold their manhood's cheap, while any speaks, that
fought with us, upon Saint Crispin's day.'

William Shakespeare, 'Henry V'

TO CATCH A FOX
Prologue
Spring 2008

Dimitri Mikhailovich Orlov sat at the big desk that had once belonged to Winston Churchill. Reflecting on the nights events, he couldn't believe what had happened. How was it possible? He was a multibillionaire, Russian oligarch and yet his daughter had just been kidnapped, from his own private island. They had captured one of the kidnappers, but the other two had escaped with his beautiful Nicole. He pressed a concealed button on the underside of the desk and silently a small secret drawer slid open. Removing the revolver, he felt the weight in his hand, as he considered his next actions.

Dimitri's two armed guards had taken the kidnapper Farad, to the maintenance building at the rear of the island. The young Arab kidnapper had soiled himself during the interrogation and now sat in a chair, still wearing the urine-soaked undershorts and T-shirt. Dimitri's men stood as their boss entered the room. The kidnapper looked afraid, but defiant; as Dimitri approached him, gun in hand. The chromed revolver glinted in the fluorescent lights, as he raised it to the head of the trembling man.

'Your friends took my daughter. Whether she lives or dies, will no longer matter to you. You will die tonight.'

He pulled the hammer back, cocking the powerful handgun, as Farad's eyes caught his. *He's not afraid to die*, thought Dimitri and lowered the weapon from the shaking man's head. He turned to his men, 'Take him as far out to sea as you can. Then throw him over the side. If he dies or lives, it will be his God who decides. Just make sure you go far enough out, so the latter does not happen.'

One security man waved his pistol indicating the kidnapper to stand, as the other roughly pulled him from the chair, twisting his arm up his back. Dimitri watched them manhandle him from the room and out to the small dock, where the service boat was moored. Pushing Farad onto the boat, the bigger of the two men waved his gun again, indicating the kidnapper to move to the bow, as the other started the engine. The mooring lines were released and Dimitri watched as the small boat disappeared into the darkness.

Although the night was warm, Farad was still shaking; his eyes darted around the small boat, assessing his options. He quickly realised their intention when, after thirty minutes of sailing, the boat slowed to a stop. The man with the weapon stood and moved towards him, indicating with the gun for him to stand. Farad did as he was directed. The man gestured to the sea, turned to his companion for a moment, grinning, but in that that split second Farad lunged with all his strength. The gun fell to the deck; the guard lost his balance and toppled over the side, cursing in Russian as he hit the water. The second man came at Farad, but he wasn't fast enough. He stopped and slowly raised his hands. The kidnapper now had the gun pointing directly at him. For the first time that night Farad smiled, and then he too waved the weapon. The guard understood and jumped over the side, into the warm waters of the Gulf. The boat swayed with the current as Farad watched the two guards splashing in the water. He slowly raised the gun, and shot them both in the head. He watched as the bodies of the two Russians drifted away into the night, then turned to the control panel and checked the compass and fuel gauge. Before he'd joined the brotherhood he'd been a successful computer programmer in Damascus and he was confident he could roughly calculate his current position. There were more than three quarters of a tank of fuel and, from the position of the moon, he assumed they'd been travelling in a north-westerly direction. If he headed due south he should hit the island of Abu al Abyad, before he ran out of diesel. He checked a storage locker at the side of the control panel and found some life-vests, two sets of clean coveralls and several bottles of water, 'Allah o' Akbah,' he said quietly, before gulping down a full litre bottle of the refreshing liquid. He removed the filthy T-shirt and undershorts and threw them over the side, took another bottle of water and washed his hair, face and torso. The coverall was far too big for him, but the clean material next to his skin revived his spirts slightly. He pressed the starter button and the engine gurgled into life. He turned the wheel to compass bearing one eight zero degrees then pushed the throttle forward to seventy percent power, steadying himself as the bow lifted and the boat gained speed.

According to the clock on the control panel he'd been sailing for an hour and a quarter when he saw lights from the island dead ahead. *Praise be to Allah*, he thought. Fifteen minutes later he cut the engine and allowed the craft to gently roll ashore on the current. The bow hit the beach and he lurched forward against the impact. He took another bottle of water from the locker and jumped from the boat onto the soft sand, just as the sun was rising.

Two hundred metres along the beach was a small cluster of houses, with several fishing boats pulled up along the shoreline. He set off towards them and a few minutes later saw a young man leave one of the buildings.

'Salam Alaikum,' shouted Farad.

'Alaikum Salam,' replied the young man.

'My name is Farad, can you help me please, brother? I was on a boat that sank and I have only just managed to get to this blessed shore,' he continued.

'How can I help you?' said the man.

'May I use a phone and can you tell me where I am, please?'

The man took out a cell phone and handed it to Farad, 'You are on Abu Al Abyad,'

'Praise, Allah,' said Farad, 'and the name of this village?'

'This is Al Ruam.'

Farad took the cell phone and punched in the number; after several rings a sleepy voice said, 'Yes?'

'Salam Alaikum, this is Farad, sir. There has been a serious problem and I've been separated from my brothers.'

'Where are you?'

'I'm on Abu Al Abyad, sir, at a village on the coast, called Al Ruam.'

'Hold the line.'

Farad could hear muffled voices on the other end and then, 'Stay there. Do not move or talk to anyone. Someone will be with you in a few hours.'

'Thank you, sir.'

The line went dead.

Chapter One
Spring 2009

The date on the newspaper read 9th March 2009. As the camera focus moved to wide angle, the picture blurred for a few seconds and then cleared. Jack Castle held the paper in front of him. His right hand was wrapped in a bloody, dirty bandage. The left side of his face was purple and bruised and his eye was closed and swollen. He wore a shabby white coverall, with several blood stains on the front. His hair was greasy and matted and his jawline was covered by several days of beard growth. His bare feet were filthy and the soles left bloody marks on the cold concrete floor. The right eye was wide open and although bloodshot, held a gaze of defiance. He was flanked by two men dressed in black T-shirts and black denims. The shirts were emblazoned with Arabic Cyrillic and their faces were obscured by black kufiyahs. The light from the video camera reflected on their fake Ray Ban sunglasses.

'My name is Jack Castle. I am a British mercenary and infidel. I am being held by the Islamic State for Iraq and the Levant. I am being treated well.' He raised his right eyebrow, then gave a pronounced wink to the camera, smiled slightly, and continued.

'I will be released in good health once the following ransom has been paid.' Jack coughed, holding his ribs, he coughed again and winced. He took a deep breath, ignoring the pain and continued. 'The ransom will be in two parts. First: fifty million dollars, to be considered as reparation for the ISIL brothers I murdered. Second: twenty million dollars will secure my full release. Payment will be made into multiple intermediary bank accounts, of which details will be provided by email, in the next twenty four hours. The deadline for payment is six days from today. If the ransom is not paid by noon on the fifteenth, I will be executed on camera.'

The spotlight was switched off and Jack was roughly pulled from his seat and taken from the room. He was dragged back to his cell and pushed in; the steel door clanging loudly as the men slammed it behind them. He raised two fingers and shouted 'Bastards,' at the closed door. He sat down on the thin grubby mattress that served as a bed and wrapped the old course rug around his shoulders. He wasn't cold, but the rug provided him some comfort in the unwelcoming cell. *It's a year since we tangled with these fuckers and they're still looking for revenge,* he thought. Then chuckling to himself, *Demanding seventy million? Yeah, right! As if they're likely to get that. Muppets!*

He removed the stale slice of Pitta bread he'd concealed under the mattress, broke off the hard edge and used it to 'clean' his teeth, then spat into the open toilet in the corner. Saying out loud, 'Right, that's me cleaned up for the day, now for some lunch,' he began chewing on the tasteless piece of food.

In his early fifties, Jack Castle was tall, reasonably fit and healthy. Greying hair complemented sparkling brown eyes that gave a light to his tanned face. He had a good sense of humour and an infectious personality that most people liked. His happy childhood had been spent in England's Lake District and he was the elder of two brothers. His father and mother had been doctors in little town of Windermere and it was his father who had taught Jack the meaning and value of responsibility, loyalty and honour. Love, kindness and respect, were the gifts his mother had endowed him with. His parents had tragically died in a car accident when he was twenty and it was this which caused Jack to abandoned the idea of becoming a doctor; electing to join the British Army instead. He'd spent fifteen years in the military trying to overcome the guilt and anger he harboured following the death of his parents. He'd worked hard and rose to the rank of captain in the Special Air Service, after which his friend Tom Hillman, had convinced him private security was the way forward and in 1993 Jack began working with Tom as personal protection officers, for high paying clients. Ten years on and it was Jack who owned the security company, with several key contracts in various conflict zones across the world. In 2003 they had set up in Baghdad and had secured a dozen major clients in Iraq and Kurdistan, as well as undertaking ad-hoc security work for the American Military. And now, here he was, kidnapped and a prisoner in a cell somewhere in the Middle East.

Chapter Two
'6 Days to go'

Tom had watched in silence as the video played out and smiled briefly when his friend winked to camera. When the short film ended he stood up and walked over to the big windows of Dimitri's study. He looked out over the crescent bay of Orel Island and thought how beautiful it was here.

'So, Tom, what do you think?' said Dimitri.

Tom turned and looked at the old Russian, then across the room to his beautiful daughter Nicole. He walked over and knelt in front of her, taking her hand he said, 'We're gonna get your husband back, Nikki, I promise.'

He'd known Nicole Elizabeth Orlov, ever since Jack had met her in Moscow, over fifteen years before. Her English mother had died when she was quite young and her father Dimitri had raised her. Back then she was a successful international model and extremely beautiful; the ensuing years had not diminished her beauty.

'He looked so bad, Tom.'

'He's tough, Nikki. You saw him wink?'

'Yes, yes.' She gave a tiny laugh through the tears, then asked, 'Will we have enough time, to get him back in six days?'

'I'm gonna start making calls right now. We'll get him.'

'What do you need from me, Tom?' said Dimitri.

'Let me make the calls first, Mitri. Then I'll go through the basis of a plan.'

Tom Hillman was Jack Castle's closest friend and business partner; they had met over twenty years ago in the Balkans. Tom was with Military Intelligence and had been attached to Jack's SAS team to neutralise an Armenian warlord, who'd been operating independently on the Armenian, Kosovo border. The mission had resulted in the warlord being killed by a single shot from Tom, a result both men thought highly appropriate, given the Armenian's history for killing refugees. They had been friends and colleagues ever since.

Tom was a few years younger than Jack, slightly shorter and slimmer, with close cropped fair hair, tanned face and blue eyes. Born in the UK, he'd spent most of his younger life in Leeds. He had two daughters from a previous marriage, but his home now was Dubai, where he lived with his second wife Helen.

* * *

Daniel Chaplain had worked with Jack in Baghdad. In his late forties, with short brown hair and brown eyes; he occasionally walked with a slight limp, from a wound he had sustained at Goose Green, during the Falklands conflict. Born in Newcastle he was a proud Geordie and strong family man, with two teenage sons. His military career had been in the Parachute Regiment, which made him a very capable man on the street, with a heart like a lion in the toughest of situations. Everyone called him Danny, unless they were taking the piss, and then he got Daniel. He'd retired from private security work, thanks to his share of the vast fortune they had realised from the Iraq mission, almost a year before. He was also one of Jack and Tom's closest friends.

The smartphone beeped just as he took his swing, causing the ball to fall short and drop spectacularly into the lake.

'Shit!'

'Jesus, Danny, you always leave your bloody phone on.'

'Sorry, guys,' he said as he looked at the caller display, 'I need to take this.'

He walked away from the three men and touched the screen, 'Tom. How're you doing, mate?'

'I'm good, Danny, but Jack has a serious problem. We need you in Abu Dhabi, fast.'

'How fast?'

'Yesterday. Can you contact Santosh and get to the VIP Lounge at Stanstead Airport, by noon tomorrow?'

'Sure, no problem.'

'Okay good. Dimitri will send his plane to pick you up. Text me soon as you've contacted, Santosh.'

'Will do. What's it all about, Tom?'

'Not over the phone. I'll see you on Orel Island tomorrow. Any idea where Steve is?'

'He's in Bangkok.'

'Okay, cheers. See you tomorrow, Danny.'

The line went dead. Danny turned to his fellow golfers, 'Sorry, guys, I gotta go.'

* * *

In South East Scotland, it was pouring with rain. Ian Andrew Little stood under a tartan umbrella, shouting at the men on the hotel roof. His bare legs under the kilt were wet and cold and he was not happy with the builder's progress on the roof. He'd bought the 16th century, country house property six months ago, with money from his share of the Iraqi diamond haul. They were half way through a two million pound refurbishment, which was taking too long and costing far more than it should, making him extremely pissed off.

Ian had been Jack's medic and communications specialist, during the search for the Iraqi treasure and like Danny, was a close friend and valued colleague of Jack's. Born in one of the better areas of Edinburgh and a young-looking forty, he was tall with black hair and dark eyes, always immaculately turned out, with a cutting sense of humour and a kind heart. He was unmarried and lived with his gay partner in their new hotel, on the outskirts of Edinburgh.

He ignored the beeping smartphone in his pocket and continued his tirade on the rooftop workers. The persistent ringing of the phone eventually made him remove the annoying instrument from his raincoat pocket. Not looking at the screen, he flipped the phone on and said in a not too pleasant voice, 'Aye?'

'Ian. It's, Tom.'

'Tom, hello there.' he replied in a friendlier tone. 'How ye dooin?

'I'm good, I'm good. But I need you down here in AD.'

'Sorry, Tom, but I'm up tae ma ears in butch builders here.'

'It's Jack. He's in serious trouble.'

'What's up?'

'Too much to say over an open line. But it's bad.'

'Okay, I'll see how quickly I can get a flight.'

'Dimitri is sending his plane. Get to Stanstead Airport by noon tomorrow. Meet Danny and Santosh at the VIP lounge. Okay?'

'Aye, I'll be there. See ye tomorra, Tom.'

Tom turned to Dimitri and Nicole, 'Okay that's the guys in the UK. I need to get hold of Steve now. Then we can go through a plan.'

Steve Shelby was born and raised in London, until he joined the army at sixteen. A couple of years younger than Jack, he was an imposing figure, tall and muscular; who'd used his physique to advantage, when playing rugby for the Parachute Regiment. Steve and Danny were friends who had met and served together in the Falklands. Steve had lost an eye at Goose Green, while rescuing Danny from an exposed position; he always played down the rescue of his friend, but everyone knew Steve had saved Danny's life. Occasionally he used a glass eye, but most of the time he wore an eye- patch. He'd invested several million dollars of his share of the Iraqi diamond money into five holiday resorts along Pattaya Beach, in Thailand and although now more of a business man than a soldier, still kept himself in good physical condition.

Tom had three numbers for Steve, only after the third, did he get an answer.

'Hallo?' It was a woman's voice, obviously Thai.

'Hi. Is Steve there please?'

'Hee sleeeping.'

'Please could you wake him? It's very important. Tell him it's Tom.'

'Wait pleeese.'

'Hello?'

'Stevie, it's Tom.'

'Hey, Tom, good to hear from you.'

'Yeah, how you doin Steve?'

'I'm good, been drinkin a bit too much, but no worries.'

'You fit?'

'Yeah. I'm not too bad really, been swimming every day. But why all the interest in my health?' he said laughing.

'Jack's in trouble, big time. I need you here, on Orel.'

'What's happened?'

'Not over the phone, Steve.'

'Okay. Right, what time is it?'

'It's just after four pm here. So, seven o-clock with you.'

'Errmm, okay. I'll see if I can get on the midnight flight to Dubai. If not I'll try the morning one to Abu Dhabi. Either way, I'll be there sometime tomorrow.'

'Great, cheers, Steve. Text me when you have flight details. Dimitri will send Mike to pick you up in the chopper, from Dubai or AD airport.' Tom looked at Dimitri, who nodded affirmation.

'Okay cool, see you soon, Tom. Bye.'

Tom went over to the window and looked out at his boat moored against the marina jetty. He'd been out on the Gulf when Dimitri had called and he'd sailed straight down to Dimitri's island. His wife Helen and the other couple had reluctantly left the beautiful island on the shuttle boat to the mainland and had been driven back to Dubai in Dimitri's Bentley. Tom's smartphone beeped and he read the text message from Danny, *Santosh & Me ok for Stnstd tomoz.* Tom confirmed receipt of the text and then turned to Dimitri, 'That's the guys on their way, they'll all be here tomorrow.'

'Good, Tom. What do we do now?' said Dimitri.

'I want to verify his location with the tracker signal and look at the video again. Then I could do with a sandwich and some coffee, please,' he said with a smile, 'nothing else to do until the guys all get here.'

Chapter Three
'5 Days to go'

It was still dark when the cell door clanged open. He hadn't been asleep, but it startled him never the less. The guard, who'd taken his Rolex on the first day, came in with a tin bowl of food and dropped it in front of Jack, spilling most of it on the dirty concrete floor. He dropped a small bottle of water next to the food and walked out, slamming the heavy metal door as he left.

'Thank you,' shouted Jack, 'this looks delicious.'

He lifted the corner of the mattress and used the small piece of stone to scratch another short line, next to the other two, on the floor. *Three days since I was taken*, he thought. *Dimitri won't go to the authorities; he'll contact Tom and the guys. Nikki will have him contact Tom.* He rubbed the inside of his thigh and imagined he could feel the embedded tracker pulsing, sending out the GPS signal of his location. *Thank fuck these muppets don't know about this.*

As the sun rose, it shone through the barred window, sending a shaft of dust filled light across to the opposite side of the cell. The sunlight lifted his spirits for a few seconds and he grinned. Disregarding the shitty accommodation and the poor food, they had not really tortured or interrogated him. He'd fought the three men who'd snatched him from outside the hotel and his injuries to face and ribs were the result. His hand had been caught when they slammed the van door shut; he was sure there were no broken bones, but it was very badly bruised and cut. The three inch gash didn't look good and he was concerned about infection, so he used half his bottled water each day, to clean the wound. He'd been in plenty of fights before and wasn't too worried about the facial bruising which, although serious at the time, always healed. He'd checked his cheek bone and eye socket and as painful as it was to touch, didn't feel like they were broken. His ribs, after the kicking, were sore and his torso badly bruised, but he didn't think there was any real damage.

The cell was twelve feet square, with concrete floor and walls. The wooden roof looked inviting and he knew he could easily escape through it, but only if he had a ladder. The open toilet in the corner did not smell as bad as when he'd first arrived, but maybe he was just getting used to it. There seemed to be no rats or insects, other than a few flies and the mattress, although filthy was not infested. Looking around the room again and enjoying the brief shaft of sunlight, he smiled and thought, *Not bad accommodation at all really*, and then tucked into his unpleasant breakfast.

* * *

The words were being spoken quietly and calmly, but the voice speaking had a sound as though coming from a grave. Listening to the voice was chilling; the sound of the words seemed to carry the blackness of death from the speaker.

'What is his condition?'

'He is in good health, Sir, he resisted when being taken and sustained some minor injuries, but nothing serious.'

'I do not want him harmed. Do you understand? No mistreatment.'

'Yes, Sir.'

'If he has need of medical assistance give it to him. I want him well for my arrival.'

'I understand, Sir.'

'I will be there the day before the deadline.'

The phone went dead.

Chapter Four
'Putting the band back together'

The engines shut down and the sleek Orel Corporation executive jet came to a stop. Santosh Nishaad looked through the window at the other private jets and planes in the Abu Dhabi VIP aircraft holding area and he thought how his life had changed since meeting Jack Castle almost five years before.

He was born in Kerala, Southern India; in his mid-thirties he'd served in the Indian Army for several years, before taking the Baghdad contract and had worked with Jack for almost five years as a driver, interpreter and fixer. Tall, with a pleasant face and huge smile; he worked out relentlessly in his hi-tech home gym. He was extremely reliable and loyal, with an inherent talent for languages, one of which was Arabic.

After the Iraqi diamond pay-out, he had bought a large country house in Berkshire and moved his wife and two sons from India, along with his mother and mother-in-law; a decision he sometimes regretted, as there were now three women constantly nagging him. He had used his money wisely and had set up several farms in Kerala, as well as buying-up every piece of land he could in his home town. He knew he owed all his success to Jack Castle and if Jack needed help, then he would be there.

The luxury shuttle bus pulled up alongside the gleaming jet with the eagle's head, Orel Corporation's logo, resplendent on the fuselage and tail.

'Here we go again,' said Danny, as he walked down the short flight of steps from the plane.

'I have a wee feelin this is gonna be a lot worse than last time,' said Ian sombrely.

The three men boarded the small coach, as a uniformed attendant took their luggage from the stewardess and loaded it into the rear compartment. The doors closed and the air-conditioning kicked in, chilling the interior to a pleasant eighteen centigrade.

After going through passport procedures in the small VIP building, they re-boarded the shuttle bus and were driven across to the helicopter pad, where Dimitri's Eurocopter was waiting. They pulled up close by the sleek helicopter and as they exited the bus Danny said, 'I had one of these.'

'Aye, for aboot about five minutes, until yer wife sent it back!' laughed Ian. Santosh joined in with the laughter, promoting a, 'Get stuffed,' from Danny.

The chopper pilot came from the other side of the aircraft and said,' Hello, gentlemen, good to see you all again. I think?'

'Hi, Mike, good to be back,' said Danny as he shook Mike's hand.

'Hullo, Mike,' said Ian, as they shook hands.

Santosh flashed the big smile, offered his hand, and nodded, 'Hi.'

The wild bunch is back, thought Mike.

'Is Steve here yet, Mike?' said Danny.

'He arrives into AD in about two hours. I'll go and pick him up, after I drop you gentlemen off on Orel Island.'

'Looks like we're putting the band back together,' quipped Danny, as he climbed into the luxurious helicopter.

* * *

It was getting dark and the sun was setting out on the Gulf, as the five men took their seats in Dimitri's home cinema. The group watched the short film in silence; with the exception of Danny, who quietly mumbled death threats and curses at the people who had taken his friend. The screen went blank and the room was silent for a few moments.

'Any questions?' said Tom.

'When do we leave?' said Steve.

Tom stood and walked to the table set with coffee and sandwiches. He took a bottle of expensive mineral water and swilled down half of it, then turned to his friends.

'It's a bit more complicated than that, guys.'

'How's that Tom? We know where he is. We have his tracker signal loud and clear. Let's just go get him and waste any bastard that tries to stop us.' demanded Steve with conviction.

'I agree,' said Danny.

'Okay, okay. Calm down. Your loyalties are not in question; otherwise you wouldn't be here. But there's a lot more involved than Jack being taken and held for ransom. Storming in there, without knowing the opposition's strength is stupid, you guys know that,'

'How'd they manage to capture the boss anyway?' said Santosh.

'And where the hell was he tae put himself in that position?' continued Ian.

Dimitri waked into the cinema; everyone stood and turned to the old Russian.

'Please. Sit down, gentlemen.' he said as he took a seat, 'I'm not too early am I, Tom?'

'No, Mitri. I'm just about to tell the guys the story and the plan.'

The room was silent, as Tom stood in front of the screen, 'About a month ago Jack was contacted by an old friend from MI6. Apparently GCHQ at Cheltenham, had picked up several signals between two or three high value ISIL targets.'

'Everyone knows GCHQ listens to everything that's of value, same as the CIA does. But what's that got to do with Jack?' said Steve.

'Let him continue please,' said Dimitri, nodding to Steve.

'As I said, they'd picked up the messages from a couple of smartphones they had homed in on. The CIA had picked up the same chatter and both agencies confirmed the identities of the targets doing the talking.'

'So who were they an what're they talking aboot?' said Ian.

'They were talking about us!'

'What the ...?' started Danny, as Tom raised his hand.

'They mentioned Jack Castle by name, but as yet, they don't know our identities. Only that we were with Jack during the encounter at the oasis, when we found the diamonds, and also the rescue mission in the gulf. They hold Jack, all of us, responsible for the killing of their men, specifically two brothers, who were the sons of the target being monitored.'

'So who is this, guy, this target?' said Santosh.

'He's a brilliant physicist and mathematician; he used to teach at the University of Damascus. His name is Professor Hassan Al Hamady and he's second in command of ISIL. His code name is Al Tha'laab.'

'The Fox!' translated Santosh.

'That's right. His sole mission is to plan and facilitate terrorist action anywhere in the world. And we killed his two sons.'

'So he's out for revenge?' said Danny.

'He wants the ransom money, but killing all of us, and our families, is top of his personal wish-list.'

'And now he's got Jack, he'll torture him to get our identities?' said Steve.

'The boss wont crack,' said Santosh.

'Everybody cracks eventually,' said Tom, 'but we don't really need to worry about that for the moment.'

'And why's that?' said Ian.

'Because Jack is right where we want him to be!'

'Are you serious?' said Danny as he stood up to get a drink.

'Carry on, Tom,' said Dimitri.

'They won't harm him, until they get the ransom, that's their top priority. The Fox wants the money to fund his worldwide campaign.'

'But there's no way any government would pay that much money,' said Steve.

'That's right. But a billionaire Russian oligarch, whose son-in-law has been kidnapped and whose daughter is at risk, would. That's why the video was sent to Mitri.'

'Hold on a wee minute. Ye said Jack was right where ye want him t'be,' said Ian.

Tom finished off his water and walked over for another bottle, 'Yes, he is. As I said earlier, Jack's pal from MI6, along with a CIA operative....,'

'Fucking spooks!' interrupted Danny, with obvious disdain.

'Quiet, Dan,' said Steve

Tom smiled at Danny's dislike of the covert services and continued, 'They came to see him and told him about a plan to kidnap him and eventually kill us and our families. The security services don't really give a toss about Jack or us. But they wouldn't stand by and let a ransom like that be paid to these bastards. Plus the chance to capture or kill The Fox is something they don't want to pass-up.'

'If they know where this Fox is, why don't they just take him out with one of these new drones they are using now? Send the bastard off to meet his seventy virgins,' said Steve.

A ripple of laughter went round the group, lightening the moment for a few seconds.

'They could never be sure of killing him. Just like Bin Laden, he's always on the move. So Jack came up with this plan to be kidnapped; knowing full well that wherever they take him, The Fox would come to him. He'd want to kill Jack himself, once the ransom had been paid and information about us had been extracted, of course.'

'So the boss is gonna kill The Fox?' said Santosh.

'No. The deal is we're going to capture and hand him over to the CIA, when we rescue Jack.'

'I know the Americans won't go after Jack and neither would the Brits, so it's up to us. But why should we bother bringing The Fox out for the Yanks?' said Steve.

'They want to know what the bastard's been planning. They believe ISIL could become a bigger threat than Al Qaeda and they want this guy as badly as they want Bin Laden.'

'With respect, that's not our concern, let them worry about that. We need to focus on getting the boss back,' interrupted Steve.

'True, but we also need their help. We can do the business, but we need the logistical and tactical support, that only the Yanks can give us in that region,' continued Tom, 'and don't forget, this guy wants us all dead. If we don't capture or kill him this time and he gets away, we're back to square one and the threat still hangs over us all.'

'Hold on. Re-wind a minute,' said Danny, 'you're telling me Jack planned this and actually let himself get kidnapped, so he could stop these bastards killing us?'

'Pretty much, yeah,' said Tom.

Chapter Five
'The Fox'

Professor Hassan Al Hamady began his academic career at Damascus University. After five years, he moved to England; swiftly earning his professorship at Cambridge. His international career took him to Harvard, where he lectured for ten years and became world renowned for his work in the field of quantum physics. At forty years old he returned to Damascus and took up a chair at his old Alma Mater, with the sole desire of educating his own people.

In 2005 his wife had been killed in a peaceful anti-government protest. This catalysis turned the peace loving husband and father, into a resentful, bitter and vengeful being. It was then he'd been approached by the newly formed radical group, who called themselves ISIL.

He was born fifty years ago, into a middle class family in Damascus, where his father and mother had been teachers. Tall and thin with long grey hair and grey straggly beard; his piercing blue eyes belied his heritage, making him look more Circassian than Arab. An attack by a feral dog when he was seven had cost him the small finger of his right hand and left him with a large cluster of scars on the right side of his neck. The lower part of his right ear was missing, torn off, when his father had dragged the animal from his screaming son.

He was reading the Quran when there was a quiet knock on the door, 'Yes?'

'Salam, Sir, please excuse me.'

'Yes, what is it?'

'We need to make preparations for your safe journey to Al Raqqahh, Sir, when will you go?'

'I wish to be there the day before the deadline.'

'Very well, Sir. May I ask how long you intend to stay?'

'Events will dictate how long, Inshallah.'

'Yes, Sir, Inshallah.'

'Do you need anything, Sir?'

'Some food after prayers.'

'Yes of course, Sir.'

The door closed and The Fox continued reading.

* * *

Nicole Orlov entered the cinema and the five men stood to greet her. 'Hello everyone,' she said in a quiet voice, 'I am so glad to see you all here. I just wish it were under happier circumstances.'

She embraced each of the men in turn kissing cheeks and hugging her husband's friends. She wore flat slip-on sandals, denim jeans with ripped knee's, a white T-shirt under a loose silk blouse. Her blonde hair was pulled back in a ponytail and she wore no makeup. There were dark circles below the beautiful eyes, which were red with crying. She held back the tears as she spoke to the men. 'I know the only people in the world who can get Jack out alive are, you. I know you will save him. Thank you, with all my heart for coming.'

Dimitri stood and embraced his daughter, then said, 'Try and get some rest darling, we have everything in hand here. The guys will be leaving tomorrow. You will see them before they go.'

'Yes of course, I know you will have a lot to plan. Good night everyone and thank you again,' she smiled briefly and left the cinema.

Tom raised his hand and nodded towards the back of the cinema. A few seconds later the screen was filled by a grainy picture of a small compound with a large central building and a couple of smaller adjacent buildings. The GPS co-ordinates indicted its position on the southern edge of the city.

'We got this from the CIA earlier today. It's a shot from a satellite over Syria. The town is called Al Raqqahh and this is the place,' said Tom, as he pointed to the screen, 'where Jack is being held.'

Forty five minutes later, fresh sandwiches, coffee and fruit were brought into the cinema. No one wanted a formal meal and no one even mentioned a drink. Each man was totally focussed on what had to be done and now Tom's plan had been discussed, each knew their responsibilities.

'Tell us about this knockout gas?' said Steve.

'Kolokol-1, codename, KO-1, is a derivative of the opiate, fentanyl. It was the gas the Russians used on the Chechens, in the 2002 Moscow theatre siege. It's virtually instantaneous and renders the victim unconscious for seven to twelve minutes, depending on the individual's physical condition. So we'll have no more than five minutes to find Jack and The Fox, exit the building and blow the charges. There are some mild short term side effects…'

'Such as?' interrupted Ian.

'Dizziness, nausea and temporary blindness; all of which clear within several minutes of breathing fresh air or taking pure oxygen,' continued Tom.

Santosh raised his hand and Tom said, 'Santosh?'

'Where're we gonna get this gas?'

'Dimitri has contacts in the FSB, the Russian Intelligence Service. There's a case with a dozen canisters on its way here as we speak. It'll arrive during the night.'

'Any other questions?' said Tom.

No reply from the group other than heads being shaken.

'Okay guys, we have an early start in the morning, so maybe a good idea to get some rest. Zero-five-hundred for breakfast in the dining room. Is that okay, Mitri?'

'Yes, of course. Food will be ready for you before you leave in the morning.'

'Right, that's it.' said Tom.

Chapter Six
'Off to Erbil'

The mood at breakfast was serious, but bullish as the guys helped themselves to a splendid breakfast from an over-stocked self-service buffet. Nicole and Dimitri had joined them in the elegant dining room, but neither took any food other than coffee. Mike, Dimitri's chopper pilot entered, 'Excuse me, sir.'

'Yes, Mike?' said Dimitri.

'We're ready to leave in fifteen minutes, sir. The flight plan for the jet to Kurdistan has now been approved and we have landing clearance from the airport at Erbil.'

'Very good. Thank you, Mike.' replied the old Russian.

'Right, gentlemen. Time to rock'n'roll,' said Tom, 'let's go get our boy back.'

Every one stood and then watched as Danny shovelled down the last of the bacon and eggs from his plate. 'When you're ready of course, Daniel,' said Steve to his friend. A ripple of laughter went round the room, as Danny stood up, chomping on a slice of toast.

'This'll be the last decent food for days,' said Dan as he spoke with a full mouth, spraying crumbs all over Santosh.

'Oh, thanks a lot, Danny,' said Santosh, as he brushed the food debris from his shirt. More laughter, then the mood turned to business once more. They all shook hands with Dimitri in turn. Nicole hugged each of the men; the huge eyes still red with tears and as she held onto Tom, said quietly, 'Please bring him back.'

Tom looked at his best friend's wife the face pale and drawn, 'We'll get him, Nikki, I promise. We'll get him.'

She leant against him, kissed his cheek, then smiled, but her eyes were void of any joy.

As Tom left the room he turned to Dimitri and nodded, Dimitri raised his hand and said, 'Good luck and God speed.'

The group left the beautiful mansion and piled into a small convoy of golf carts, for the short drive to the helipad at the tip of the island. The sun was up and the clear spring morning was getting warm. At the helipad the men quickly dismounted the carts and climbed into the opulent helicopter, Danny sitting up front with Mike, in the co-pilot's seat.

After going through the start-up and clearance protocol, the big rotors began to turn and cut into the air as the speed increased.

'Everyone good to go?' said Mike. The helicopter left the pad, and hovered for a few seconds as he increased power lifting the aircraft from the island. He turned away to starboard and swung the chopper round in a circle as he climbed into the clear morning sky, then levelling off; he flew past the beautiful mansion in the centre of Orel. Dimitri and Nicole waved from the huge veranda as the aircraft passed then disappeared towards Abu Dhabi.

Twenty minutes later the helicopter touched down at the private aircraft area of Abu Dhabi airport. The guys were met by a pretty Asian attendant who welcomed them aboard the coach. After their luggage was transferred, Mike shook hands with each man and wished them, 'Good luck.'

The coach took them to the small VIP immigration building for passport control. Garry, Dimitri's other pilot was waiting and greeted them as they entered the lounge.

'Good morning, gentlemen. We need to board the aircraft straight away please, as our take-off slot is in thirty minutes.'

Passports were processed and they left the building, climbing back onto the coach they made the short drive out to the flight line. They were greeted by the co-pilot and stewardess, as they boarded the beautiful aircraft. On any other occasion this would be a source of fun and pleasure, but this trip would not be either. Each man knew they would be in harm's way, but were committed to the plan and confident of success. If they failed not only would Jack die, but their families too, would be forever in danger from The Fox.

As they strapped into the big comfortable seats the stewardess offered them champagne, fruit juice and water. No one took champagne. There were no remarks about the stewardess ample bosom, nor her appealing bottom in the tight skirt. Steve leaned over and stretched out his open hand to Danny across the aisle. Danny winked and slapped the up-turned palm.

Ian, in the front seat, turned back to his friends and said, 'If we get oot a'this in one piece, it's gonna be a miracle.' Then in a dreadful singing voice, sang the words to the old 'Hot Chocolate' hit, 'but I believe in miracles.'

Danny joined in with the song, 'you sexy thing, you!'

Everyone laughed and the tension was broken.

Once the aircraft was in the air, Danny, Santosh and Ian quickly fell asleep. Steve and Tom moved to the rear of the cabin as the stewardess brought them coffee and a small tray of Danish pastries. Tom spoke quietly, 'How you feeling about this?'

'I'm good,' answered Steve, 'it's a good plan. Not perfect. But a good plan today is better than a perfect plan tomorrow, eh?'

Tom smiled at the old military saying, then continued, 'And if the Yanks get us out like they're supposed to, then we could be home and dry without too much heartache.'

'Yeah, I think we should be ok,' said Steve, 'it's getting in with the surprise element in-tact, that's the key and quickly locating Jack and this tosser, the Fox. He'll be hard to identify, even with the scarring on his neck, but no worries, we'll find the bastard.'

Two hours later the stewardess walked along the small cabin and checked everyone had their belts fastened. Garry's voice came over the speaker, 'Landing in two minutes, gentlemen.'

Santosh turned to Danny, flashed his big smile and said, 'back in the Badlands, boss!'

'Back in the Badlands, buddy,' replied Danny with a huge grin.

The aircraft banked to starboard as it made its approach to Erbil airport, then levelled off and swiftly descended onto the huge runway, touching down with an almost unperceivable bump.

As it taxied towards the main terminal, a small vehicle drove smartly in front with a FOLLOW ME sign illuminated on the roof. The jet was escorted to the farthest gate at the end of the terminal where two airport officials stood waiting, along with an American in military uniform.

As the guys disembarked, Garry shook each of their hands in turn. As Tom left the plane he said, 'Thanks' Garry, you have a safe flight back.'

The pilot held onto his hand for a few moment and looking Tom in the eyes said, 'I don't know what you guys are up to here, but it's gotta be something pretty serious, so good luck and be safe.'

The group walked over to the small welcoming party, as their luggage was quickly off-loaded. The smart looking soldier stepped forward and said, 'Tom Hillman?'

'That's me, Captain. Good morning and this is Steve, Santosh, Ian and Danny.'

'Good morning gentlemen, we're expediting your arrival into Kurdistan as personnel attached to the US Military, but these gentlemen,' he indicated the officials, 'need to look at your passports. There will be no formal stamp, as you are not officially in-country. But they do want to verify you are who we say you are.'

Tom quickly collected the passports and handed them to the captain, who in turn passed them to the officials. As the two immigration officers flicked through the documents the soldier said, 'I'm Captain Charles Hamilton, Military Intelligence, and I'll be your liaison while you're with us, sir.'

'It's a pleasure to meet you, Captain. Please call me, Tom.'

The passports were handed back as one of the officials flicked an un-impressive salute to the captain, then turned to the group and with a wave of his arm indicated for them to leave.

Tom nodded and smiled at the officials, as Hamilton said, 'we're over here gentlemen.'

They exited through the perimeter gate at the end of the terminal and boarded two unmarked Ford 4X4's. Tom climbed in to the back of the first vehicle, with the captain, as the rest of the guys piled into the second.

'Have you been to Kurdistan before, Tom?' said the captain.

'Yes, we've a couple of small security contracts in the region, but I haven't been in Erbil for over a year.'

'Then you'll know it's only a few minutes to our base?'

'You mean the not-too-secret, secret base on the other side of the airport?' said Tom with a smile.

'Yes, just so, Tom,' replied the captain, also smiling, 'everyone knows we're here, but we do like to keep a very low profile.'

'Of course, of course,' said Tom, 'excuse my flippancy.'

'Not at all. There's a gentlemen from British Intelligence waiting for you, he arrived on the Istanbul flight, last night.'

Tom's face looked stern as he said, 'More spooks!'

'Fraid so, Tom, we're everywhere these days.'

'Sorry, Captain, I wasn't being disrespectful, in fact I was Military Intelligence, in another life.'

'Yes, I know.'

Tom looked at the young officer and smiled, 'Yes, of course you do.'

Chapter Seven
'4 Days to go'

The morning sky was clear and the air crisp and cool. Trees bordered the hillside cemetery which sloped down to the river. He stood at the top of the hill and watched as the coffin was carried from the shiny black hearse to the edge of the open grave. Dozens of floral wreaths and arrangements covered the pile of earth close by. Over a hundred family, friends and mourners stood in tightly packed order. He recognised most of the faces and was surprised to see so many from the past. He thought to go down and join them, but instead took a seat on the nearby bench and watched the proceedings from the hilltop.

The sound of the birds chirping was interrupted by the lone saxophone player. The soft deep tones making a tune he knew well, *'A Walk in the Night, by Junior Walker.'* The melodic sound sent a slight shiver through him as it brought back memories. The gathered crowd looked at each other and many smiled as the soul music reverberated down the hillside. A few closed their eyes and swayed to the rhythm of the music.

The musician finished and bowed his head in respect, as the cleric stepped forward: the crisp white cassock wafted gently in the light morning breeze. The cleric began to speak, but he was too far away to hear the words. The rest of the crowd joined in and he could hear they were praying, solemn, gentle words, meant to lift hearts' at a time such as this. Others in the crowd spoke, but again he was unable to hear their words. Something one had said caused a ripple of light laughter, which seemed to ease the sadness for a moment; solemnity swiftly returning.

The cleric was speaking again now and then the crowd began to sing. '*Jerusalem*'. The grand old hymn lifting the spirts of the singers, as they raised their voices in unison. Other people in the cemetery stopped, watched and listened, as the large crowed reached the crescendo, a few even applauded at the culmination of the song.

Through the crowd four men approached the coffin and began their gentle handling and lowering of the heavy box into the open grave. Recovering the ropes and stepping back the four disappeared into the crowd. The cleric was speaking again now and then a loud *'Amen'* from the multitude. He continued to watch from his hilltop seat as the mourners filed past the open grave, each dropping a small handful of soil or flowers on top of the box below. He stood to walk down the hill and pay his respects when a movement in his peripheral vision caused him to turn. He was surprised to see his mother walking towards him, her hand raised in a slight wave, a smile on her beautiful face.

'Hello, darling,' she said as she approached.

He hugged her and kissed her cheeks, feeling the cold of the morning on them.

'I've come to take you with me, darling.'

'Take me where?' he said.

'With me, you have to come with me.'

He looked into his mother's beautiful eyes and said 'Should I be afraid?'

'No, not you,' then slipping her arm into his said, 'time to go.'

He turned to look at the crowd below and raised his hand, but no one returned his wave.

A salt laden tear ran down the side of Jack's face and trickled into his ear, causing him to wake from the dream. He stood up from the thin mattress and rubbed his face with both hands; took a drink from the small bottle of water and thought, *Jesus, that's all I need, dreaming about my own funeral! Getta grip big man!*

Jack's thoughts were forgotten with the sound of the steel bolts being drawn. The man who'd taken Jack's Rolex came in, grinned and then ushered a woman into the room.

Outside the door, another guard stood holding an AK47. Jack could see him grinning as well.

'What the hell's this all about?' said Jack.

The woman looked fearful but stood upright, not cowed. She wore a full length bourka and a hijab that covered her hair, but not her face. She carried a small leather bag that had seen better days. Rolex guard stepped to the side, allowing the woman to enter the cell.

'My name is, Mina Siddiqi. I'm a doctor. I've been brought here to check your condition.'

Jack didn't reply. He was stunned by the strikingly beautiful eyes looking at him. He realised he was staring, maybe his mouth had fallen open, he didn't know. He looked over to Rolex man and was about to speak, when the doctor continued in perfect English, 'Don't be afraid, I'm here to examine you and treat your wounds. I'm not one of these people.'

'I'm not afraid, Doctor, just surprised.'

She turned to the guard and spoke in Arabic, 'Please bring some boiling water.'

Rolex man looked at her and ignored the order, until his comrade outside told him to do as the doctor had requested. Jack recognised the mumbled Arabic profanity, as the man left.

'Sit down please, sir'

'My name is Jack, Jack Castle.'

'Sit please, Jack,' she said with a slight smile.

She opened the bag and took out some latex gloves and put them on. After feeling around the eye and cheek she said, 'Nothing is broke here, only swelling which looks to be receding.'

'I know; I checked it a few days ago.'

He saw the little smile appear again.

'Let me look at your hand, please.'

She removed the dirty bandage, checked his fingers and wrist: then looked at the wound.

The guard returned with the water and placed it on the floor in front of the woman, splashing some on her burkah in the process. She took a small bottle of Dettol from her bag and poured all of it into the bowl. Taking Jack's hand, she gently immersed it into the water. He winced at the heat and sting of the disinfectant and Rolex man grinned. 'Leave your hand in the water please,' she said, then took a syringe from the bag along with two small clear liquid vials.

'What are they?' said Jack.

'This is anti-tetanus and this is a strong antibiotic. I am going to give you a heavy dose of both. You'll feel a little nauseous having this much in your system, but it will help you.'

'Go ahead, Doc, a little sickness is not gonna make much difference in this place.'

After administering the shots, cleaning the wound and re-dressing the hand, she said, 'Any other injuries?'

'A couple of bruised ribs, but you can't do anything about that.'

'I'll give you some painkillers.'

Then, looking into his eyes, asked, 'Anything else, sir?'

'Jack, call me, Jack.'

'Anything else, Jack?'

'No, that's it, Doc, just send your bill to my office,' he said smiling.

'Rolex man spoke, shattering the moment and the doctor said, 'He is saying that you do not recognise him, Jack.'

Jack turned and looked at the grinning guard, 'I don't know this idiot,' but then, looking into the man's eyes, there seemed to be a hint of recollection. 'Maybe I've met him somewhere. I don't know.'

Rolex spoke again, but this time there was no grin, just hatred, as he spat the words out.

'He said his name is Farad and that you captured him on an Island called Orel.'

Jack looked at the man again and realised it was the kidnapper they had interrogated the night Nicole had been taken. 'So, you escaped Dimitri's men eh? You are one lucky bastard.'

'Do you wish me to translate?'

Jack looked Farad in the eyes and said, 'No, doc, it's okay,' he held the man's stare until the guard lowered his eyes and spat on the floor. The doctor closed up her bag, but not before discreetly passing Jack a small orange. He looked at her and for a second or two, was lost for words, the simple act of kindness, and bravery on her part, touched his heart and he smiled. They both stood up and he said, 'Thank you, Doctor. You've been a ray of sunshine today.'

She nodded slightly, then as she turned to leave said, 'God protect you, Jack.'

Chapter Eight
'The Spooks'

The two 4x4's pulled up in front of a small building, that looked as if it was disused. They dismounted the vehicles and Tom said, 'This looks very homely.'

'Looks like it's ready to fall down!' said Danny.

'Sorry, gentlemen, but we thought it best to keep you away from the central accommodation area. No need to have our guys knowing you're here,' said the captain with a smile, 'but my understanding is, you won't be here long anyway?'

They picked up their bags and entered the old building. Along the inside walls were several steel framed beds with mattresses, but no bedding. In the centre of the building on two long tables were piles of equipment. Standing at the end of the hut were two men in civilian clothes, both were in their early fifties; one wore jeans and a T-shirt, the other a grey lightweight suit.

'Spooks,' said Steve.

'Aye,' said Ian.

'Be cool guys, said Tom; then walked to the end of the room with the captain.

The other four went to the centre tables and began checking the neat piles of equipment.

'Hello,' said the larger of the two civilians. Tom recognised the accent, Southern states, probably Louisiana. 'I'm Greg,' he continued.

'CIA?' said Tom.

Greg smiled and turned to the man next to him, 'This is Mathew Richmond, one of your own countrymen.'

'MI6?' said Tom, as he outstretched his hand.

'Hello, Tom, please call me Matt. Good to meet you at last. I've heard great things about you from Jack. It's a shame we can't all be meeting under more pleasant circumstances.'

'Indeed,' replied Tom.

'Okay, gentlemen,' interrupted the captain, 'if you'll excuse me, I shall leave you to conduct your business. My team is ready to transport you to the border this evening. I'll be back at eighteen hundred hours. I've arranged for meals for you and your men to be delivered here in a couple of hours, if that's okay, Tom?'

Tom shook the soldier's hand and said, 'That'll be fine, thank you, Captain,' then turning to the two men said, 'I'll just check with the guys that we have all the equipment, then we can talk.'

The three men joined the rest of the team and Tom said, 'Everything here?'

'Unmarked uniforms, boots and body armour for all of us, plus Jack, Kenny and Sarmad,' said Santosh.

'Kenny and Sarmad are the other two members of your team?' said Matt.

'Yes. We'll rendezvous on the border tonight,' answered Tom.

'We got the Mac10 machine pistols we asked for,' said Danny with obvious delight, plenty of ammo and silencers for the side-arms, all here.'

'What about our 'special' requests, Steve?' said Tom.

'Night-vision gear and gas masks are good,' then opening a short reinforced aluminium case, said, 'Oh very nice!'

'What've you got Steve?' said Danny.

'A collapsible SIG 50 sniper rifle, with German scope and silencer; lovely piece of kit.'

'Explosives?' said Tom.

'Six kilos of C4 and plenty of timer detonators,' grinned Steve.

'Medical crash-pack and oxygen, are good,' said Ian, 'and the communication gear is all top-o-the range.'

'Oxygen?' said the man from the CIA.

'There's a wee side effect tae the knock-oot gas,' said Ian, 'the oxygen'll help Jack tae recover faster.'

'Okay, understood,' said Greg; then pointing to the piles of equipment, continued, 'can we clear this table please, gentlemen?' Opening his briefcase he took out several photographs, 'these are the latest shots from the satellite.'

Tom went to his bag, returned to the table and spread out a large scale plan of the compound where Jack was being held, along with a map of the surrounding area.

'Right, Gentlemen, let's get down to business,' drawled the big American.

A knock on the door, just after thirteen hundred hours, brought the briefing to an end. Santosh opened the door and said, 'It's the food.'

'Ask them to wait a moment please, while we clear this away.' said Tom.

The maps and photographs were returned to Tom's bag, while the remainder of the equipment was moved from the central tables onto the beds.

'We'll leave you to your lunch, gentlemen.' said the American. Then, shaking hands with each man in turn said, 'Good luck. We'll see you in a few days.'

Mathew followed his American counterpart and also shook hands, saying, 'Yes indeed, we'll see you in a few days, God speed,' then turning to Tom continued, 'I'll see you off from the flight-line this evening, Tom.'

As they left the room Danny said, 'Fucking spooks!'

A ripple of laughter went round the group. 'Okay, let's see what we've got to eat,' said Steve.

After lunch, Ian set the black padded hold-all he had brought, onto the table. Carefully unzipping the bag he revealed an air-tight fibreglass case, about the size of a wine box. On the top and sides were several words in Russian Cyrillic; under which was a sinister looking skull and crossbones motif.

'Kolokol-1. Please handle carefully!' translated Tom.

'Please handle carefully? That's very polite for the bloody Russians.' said Danny.

'I wanna do a wee test on this, Tom,' said Ian, 'so I can see the side effects.'

'Right, I agree,' answered Tom, 'try it on me.'

'I think you need to see the side effects as well,' said Steve, 'try the shit on me.'

Danny had the gas-masks and as he handed one to each of his friends said, 'I'll do it.'

The rest of the guys laughed when Santosh said, 'Anything to get a kip, eh, Dan?'

They put on the masks and Ian carefully opened the case. Inside, was indeed like a wine box, with a dozen sections each holding a large silver aerosol canister. Ian carefully removed one and the same Cyrillic warning and skull motif, was emblazoned along the side. A small trigger mechanism, secured by a safety clip topped the container. With a voice like Darth Vader coming through his mask, Ian said, 'Just relax the noo, Danny, you'll no feel a thing.'

The moment Ian pressed the trigger, Danny was unconscious. 'Wow, that was fast,' said Steve.

After replacing the safety clip and returning the canister to the case, Ian said, 'Open the door and windows please, Santosh, let's get some air in here.' He went to Danny and checked his pulse, then lifted each eyelid, shining a pen-torch into the eye, and said, 'He's out cold.'

Tom had been timing the experiment and after nine minutes Danny began to stir.

'You aw' right, pal,' said Ian, as he checked Danny's pulse again.

Danny sat up and coughed, his breathing was shallow, but not cause for concern. He began to rub his eyes, and Ian said, 'Dinnae do that, just blink rapidly. Can ye see?'

Danny coughed again and replied, 'It's like a fog, can't see a fucking thing.'

'Pass me the oxygen, Santosh' said Ian

Santosh handed him the small green cylinder and Ian held the rubber facemask to Dan's mouth. 'Breathe deeply.'

Within two minutes Danny's eyesight returned and he said, 'Oh no!'

'What is it, wee man?' said Ian, an air of concern in his voice.

'Oh no, no!' said Danny again, 'I can see you, ahhhhh.'

Chapter Nine
'Blackhawk to the Border'

Tom had spent the afternoon studying the plan of the compound, the location of the compound in the city and the location of Al Raqqah in relation to the surrounding geography. They had the initial plan for the actual rescue and the extraction by US helicopters, plus a contingency if anything went wrong, but Tom, like Jack, always had at least one more contingency in the event of a total cluster-fuck. His thoughts were interrupted when Steve asked, 'You okay, boss?'

'Yes, Steve, just considering other options in case the shit hits the fan.'

Steve removed the eye patch and wiped his eyelid and cheek with a clean handkerchief.   'We have a good plan, Tom. We've surprise on our side and as long as we knock 'em all out and get away clear, we may not even have to fire a shot.'

'True, but if it does go pear shaped we could be fighting a hundred of these guys. We could be fighting the whole city'

Tom checked his watch, it was just after seventeen thirty hours when he said, 'Okay, let's get all the gear into the bags.'

After packing their civilian clothes into their personal luggage, they had changed into the black coverall uniforms, 'Do we leave our own gear here, boss?' said Santosh.

'Yeah, we'll pick it up when we get back. I'll get the captain to secure if for us.'

By ten minutes to six, all the equipment had been carefully and methodically stowed into the lightweight rucksacks. Weapons, ammunition and communications equipment had been attached securely to their body armour. They now stood around Ian, checking the read out from the tracking device. 'Jack is still in the same location he's been in for the last few days?' said Tom.

'Aye,' confirmed Ian, 'I've been monitorin the signal three times a day, since I arrived on Orel Island. The boss has nae bin moved.' He switched off the equipment and stowed it carefully into his rucksack. At two minutes to six Captain Hamilton walked in with the MI6 operative.

'Good evening, gentlemen. All good to go?'

'All good,' answered Tom.

They left the old building and climbed into the back of a large, canvas covered military truck, carefully stowing their gear along the centre of the vehicle. The MI6 man was the last to climb in. The captain stood back, as one of his men closed up the tail gate. 'It's only a few minutes to the flight line, gentlemen, so just relax.

I'll see you there,' he turned and walked to a small jeep that was parked behind the truck and got in.

The sun was setting as the truck pulled up to the edge of the helipad. Two US Marine helicopters were waiting, their rotors turning slowly. Tom and the guys offloaded their gear and stood in a line waiting for instruction from the pilot to move forward and board the nearest Blackhawk.

'Good luck again,' said the captain, as he shook Tom's hand.

'Thank you, Captain. We'll see you in a few days. We've left our personal gear in the hut, could you secure it 'til we get back please?'

'I'll take care of it, Tom.' Moving along the line, he shook each man's hand, saying, 'Good luck.'

The MI6 man stepped forward and shook Tom's hand, 'When you're ready for extraction, your call sign will be, Bulldog. The helicopters picking you up will be Maverick One and Maverick Two. That's it. Good luck and be safe, Tom. I'll see you, Jack and the guys, back here in a few days' time. The beers will be on me.'

'Bring plenty of cash then!' shouted Danny over the noise of the rotors.

The pilot waved and the group moved towards the helicopter in single file, heads bowed. Tom stood to the side, as the Marine door gunner helped Ian, Santosh,

Danny and Steve climb into the open doorway. Tom passed his gear up to Steve and turned to the men standing at the edge off the helipad. He gave a thumb's-up, which was acknowledged by raised hands from the two men. After climbing on-board, he strapped himself in next to the door, and connected his earpiece to the aircraft's internal communications system.

The pilot's voice came over the intercom, 'Good evening, gentlemen. Flight time to the border will be about thirty five minutes. I'm advised you're all familiar with this type of aircraft?' he turned and saw each man raise a thumbs-up, then continued. 'Soon as we clear the airfield, we'll be testing the door guns; this is normal procedure, please don't be concerned. Relax and enjoy the flight.'

The doors were left open, as was usual on military aircraft in this part of the world. The rotors increased speed and bit into the warm evening air. The helicopter shook and vibrated as the pilot increased power and the Blackhawk lifted slowly from the tarmac. It hovered for a few seconds and then tilted forward as it began its slow climb from the flight line. The second helicopter took off and fell into formation to the right and rear of the lead Blackhawk. The two aircraft were away from the main airstrip and out over the open countryside within five minutes, when the pilot's voice came over the intercom again, 'Weapons check. Go!'

The gunners on each door racked the cocking mechanism, pointed their weapons toward the ground and fired a couple of shorts burst. The noise from the fifty calibre machine guns firing from both doorways was almost deafening, but it didn't bother Danny, who was already asleep.

Chapter Ten
'Laurence of Newcastle'

The pilot's voice came through the intercom, 'Landing in five minutes, gentlemen. Stand-by.'

The gunners assumed alert-status on the door guns, ready for anything that might come out of the darkness below. The Blackhawk banked to the left and reduced altitude. The pilot's voice came on again, 'Looks like your guys have found us a safe place to put down. There are three strobe lights dead ahead, Going in now.'

The big helicopter reduced forward speed and began a rapid descent, kicking up a cloud of dust as its wheels touched the sand. Nothing could be seen in the darkness and then a flashlight flicked on and off, as a figure approached the helicopter. The door-gunner immediately trained his weapon on the man and then relaxed, as Tom said, 'He's one of mine.'

Tom jumped down from the open doorway and greeted the man, as the rest of the team disembarked and offloaded their equipment. The pilot leaned out of his window and gave Tom a thumbs-up, shouting something that was inaudible over the clatter of the rotors. The door gunner flicked a casual salute, as the team moved away from the helicopter. The group watched as the engines increased power and the rotors bit into the night air; then shielded their eyes, as the Blackhawk lifted off and disappeared into the Iraqi night.

The silence, after the noise of the helicopters, was a welcome relief. The group followed the new arrival and quickly covered the fifty yards from the landing zone to a cluster of derelict building. They entered a small roofless house in the centre the tiny hamlet, where another man was sitting next to a small fire. The smell of fresh coffee permeated the night air. Tom went to the fire, as the man stood up and said 'Salaam Alaikum, sidi. It's good to see you again.'

'Alaikum Salaam, Sarmad. How're you my friend?'

'I'm good, inshallah,' then both men smiled and hugged each other.

Tom turned to the other man, 'How's it going Kev?'

'Okay, boss. Good to see you all,' then after shaking hands and hugging each other said, 'wish it were under happier circumstances though!'

Kevin 'Kev' Collins and Jack had first met in Somalia, back in the days when Mohamed Farrah Aidid, was the rebel warlord controlling Mogadishu. They'd been working for rival security companies, each contracted by the United Nations to defend the food convoys. The two men had formed a friendship and had stayed in contact over the years; but it was not until 2003 when Kev and Jack had met up again. Kevin had found himself in a desperate situation after a particularly nasty divorce. Then a motorcycle accident had resulted in him being laid up for six months, with the subsequent loss of a good job in the Middle East. Kev had been in serious financial difficulties and he'd approached Jack for a position in Baghdad. Without hesitation he'd been taken on and the friendship had grown ever since. Now, six years on, Kevin was the operations manager for the company in Kurdistan and when Tom had contacted him for help, there was no hesitation that he would join the mission.

Santosh, Steve, Danny and Ian shook hands with Sarmad, then Danny said, 'fresh coffee in the middle of the desert, great stuff, Sarmad.'

Sarmad al Bazaz, had become a trusted and close friend to Jack and Tom, and indeed the rest of the guys, since joining the company in 2004. Born in Erbil, he was a devout Kurdish Muslim, with strong religious and moral beliefs. In his early forties he was in good physical condition thanks to his love of swimming. His wife of ten years had given him two sons and a daughter. He had been a biology teacher in his younger life, until being conscripted into the Iraqi army and was a respected soldier who had risen to the rank of lieutenant by the time the International Coalition entered Iraq. He'd lost his position, income and self-resect when the army, along with the police and other Iraqi security forces, were disbanded by the American Provisional Government.

After Jack met Sarmad, the two men had found a mutual respect for each other and not too long after, Jack hired him as deputy general manager of the newly formed Erbil branch of the company. The trust and position shown by Jack, had given Sarmad the chance to rebuild a life for himself and his family and the last five years had been prosperous and filled with opportunity. If Jack was in need of his help, there would be no question that Sarmad would give it.

After helping themselves to the strong coffee and finding seats on various pieces of broken masonry, the group sat quietly and listened to Tom reiterate the plan for Kevin and Sarmad. The flames from the small fire flickered on their faces, as Tom concluded the briefing, then looking at his watch, said, 'It's almost seven thirty. We should load up the beasts and get moving.'

The small ruin was plunged into darkness, as sand was kicked over the fire. Their night vision kicked in as each man took up his equipment and followed Sarmad out to the far side of the cluster of old buildings.

'Oh fuck!' said Danny, when he saw the dozen camels waiting for them.

Everyone laughed as Steve nodded towards Danny, saying, 'Laurence of Newcastle.'

Two days earlier, Sarmad had met his brother Kamal in Mosul, where they had procured the best camels that were on offer in the local market. Kevin had bought a couple of old trucks and the animals had been driven to the border rendezvous by the three men. After unloading the animals and supplies, Kamal had returned to Mosul in one of the trucks, with express instructions to say nothing of the whole escapade to anyone. And now they were ready to move. The camels were loaded with the equipment under Sarmad's supervision. One animal for each of them, plus three to carry equipment, water, and food; with a couple of spare beasts, should anything untoward happen. They would only be in the desert for two nights, so there was no great need for huge volumes of food, but it was wise to carry plenty of water. The distance from the border to Al Raqqah was over 170 miles, most of which was flat desert, with a central area of sand dunes. He knew the camels were capable of travelling at ten to twelve miles an hour across compacted sand, but half that speed over the dunes. The plan was to travel for ten or eleven hours each night, when the temperature would be kinder on the animals and the pace could be maintained, so he was confident they would be on location the night before the deadline.

As they walked the camels out of the cluster of buildings, Danny said, 'Can I ask why we aren't parachuting in, or at least driving?'

'Because the Americans wouldn't commit to an incursion over Syria to drop us,' answered Tom.

'But they're happy tae come in once we get the bloody Fox for them?' said Ian.

'Yeah, and let's hope they do, coz I don't think these smelly beasts are designed for a fast getaway.' said Santosh.

'No they aren't,' said Tom, 'but they are definitely the best way to get to Al Raqqah undetected. So mount-up and lets rock'n'roll.'

Chapter Eleven
'Desert & Dunes'

They made steady progress across the flat desert, stopping only twice during the night to rest the camels; while the team consumed energy bars and water. Just after six thirty the sun rose on the horizon behind them, sending weird shaped shadows across the desert and taking the chill from the night air.

'Okay, guys, let's stop and check the GPS, see how we've done,' said Tom.

The animals bellowed and grunted as their riders prodded them into the kneeling and then sitting positions. After dismounting, stretching backs and rubbing buttocks, Steve said, 'Oh my arse is killing me.'

'Ask Ian to give it a rub for you, darling,' said Danny effeminately.

'Fuck off, twat,' said Steve.

'Aye, fuck off,' said Ian, 'Stevie's far too butch fer me. But you're just ma type Daniel.'

The group laughed as the joke, as usual, backfired on Danny.

Ian had taken the GPS tracker from his bag and was calculating the distance from the border to their current location. Like lottery players listening for the results, the guys crowded round him, waiting for the information on the night's progress.

'Seventy five miles,' announced Ian, 'we covered seven five bloody miles last night.'

'What'd you think, Sarmad?' said Tom. 'Can we stop or do we move on for another hour or so?'

'We've made good progress, but we must rest the animals now, we drove them hard last night, so yes, we will camp here. We should leave an hour before sunset this evening and as we have the dunes to cross, the pace will not be as fast; but I believe we will still be able to travel at least fifty miles tonight.'

'And tomorrow night?' said Tom, 'ETA to Raqqah?'

'Estimated time of arrival at Al Raqqah,' said Sarmad, 'we'll be back on flat desert tomorrow night and if we leave an hour before sunset again, we should reach the outskirts of the city by o-two-hundred on the day of the deadline, inshallah.'

'Okay, gentlemen, we're on schedule, so well done,' continued Tom. 'I know it's been uncomfortable,' he said as he rubbed his backside, 'so let's get breakfast and then some sleep. I'll take the first watch and wake you in ninety minutes, Steve,'

'Okay, boss.'

In spring, the weather in Northern Syria is not that oppressive, with temperatures around twenty plus centigrade. But in the open desert and with no shade, the relentless sun is unpleasant to say the least, nevertheless, the day passed uneventfully and each of the guys took their turn on watch, although sleep was attempted, little was had. The camels were the only ones who actually slept the day away, groaning, snoring and farting, as they did so.

By late afternoon a slight wind had come up from the south, bringing with it dust and sand; not enough to obscure vision, but enough to make it uncomfortable to sit around in. So the departure was brought forward by an hour or so, and after a meal of energy bars, fruit and water, the group loaded up the beasts and continued their journey deeper into the unforgiving desert.

The further west they travelled, the less the wind blew and by the time they had reached the dunes, the wind had dropped completely. The moon was almost full and the sky, with the abatement of the wind, had become clear and full of stars.

'We've been on the move over five hours now,' shouted Sarmad, 'we should rest the animals.'

'Okay, we stop here,' confirmed Tom.

The groaning and bellowing from the camels, as they were coaxed into their sitting positions broke the silent night air. The team dismounted and walked around stretching leg and back muscles.

'This is bollocks,' said Danny.

'I quite like it, said Santosh, as he winked at Steve.

Yeah, me too,' added Steve.

'Are you fucking kiddin me?' said Dan.

'Yes!' said Steve, 'the only bloody camel I want to see after this, is sliced and grilled, on a plate with chips.'

'If mine doesn't stop farting, you could be having grilled camel for breakfast,' said Dan.

Tom smiled to himself at the banter between the men, and then said to Ian, 'how we doing distance wise?'

'Weer anither forty miles in tae the desert. But the next ten or twelve are the doons, so the pace'll drop off a wee bit.'

'It will drop off quite a lot,' added Sarmad.

'Okay, but we're making good time, right?' said Tom.

'We are doing very well,' confirmed Sarmad, with a big smile, 'maybe three or four hours across the dunes and then we rest on the other side.'

'Excellent, let's eat,' said Tom.

The caravan moved slowly westward, with the dunes proving more of a challenge than expected. Although the moon was almost full and provided good light to travel by, the soft shifting sand under the animal's hoofs slowed the pace dramatically. Even though Santosh and Danny had succumbed to the undulating movement of the camels, resulting in both being unseated, the mood within the group was positive. Spirts rose during a short break, when Ian announced they only had a few more miles of unforgiving sand hills to traverse.

It was still dark with daybreak an hour away when the desert turned from dunes to flat compact sand again.

'I think we should stop here,' said Sarmad, 'the animals have been pushed hard over the hills, they need to rest.'

'Okay,' said Tom, 'let's make camp at the base of the dune.'

'Thank fuck,' said Danny.

The beasts grunted and bellowed as usual during the ungainly ritual of assuming the sitting position, and it did not take long for the team to offload equipment, eat some food and settle down for the days sleep.

'Same watch duty as yesterday, guys?' said Tom, 'call you in ninety minutes, Steve?'

Chapter Twelve
'My Name is Hassan'

Jack hoped all had gone well with the plan he and Tom had devised before he was captured and if all had indeed gone to plan, then tonight would see him free. His thoughts of the forthcoming night's action were interrupted by the clatter of bolts and the door being unceremoniously thrown open. The guard, Jack now knew to be Farad entered; his colleague stood outside, AK at the ready. After a token kick at Jack and then in broken English, Farad said, 'You come now.'

'No, thanks mate, I've just booked a massage and she should be here any minute.'

Farad looked at the other guard for some understanding and said again, 'you come now.'

The hapless guard raised his foot to kick out again, but Jack was on his feet, 'just taking the piss mate, just taking the piss.'

The outside guard waved his weapon, as Jack walked out into the dusty corridor. The difference in temperature between his cell and the hallway was noticeable and he shivered slightly at the pleasant coolness. Farad pushed past him and led the way, the armed guard covering Jack from behind. They took him down a second hallway and stopped at a sturdy looking door. Farad knocked and waited. After a few seconds he knocked again and the door was opened by an old man in long brown robes.

'Please come in, Mr Castle.'

Jack was taken aback for a second at the perfect English spoken by the old man. It was English with the slightest hint of American accent. The man dismissed Farad with a wave of his hand. The armed guard was directed to the corner of the room in the same manner.

'Please sit down, would you like some water?'

Jack looked the man straight in the eye and said, 'water, yes please.'

The old man moved to a low table, picked up two small bottles of water, handed one to Jack, then pointing to the carpet and cushions on the floor said, 'please sit, Mr Castle.'

Sitting, and then leaning back against the wall, the old man looked at Jack for several seconds, 'my name is Hassan, Hassan Al Hamady. You are Jack Castle and you and your friends killed my two sons in Iraq.'

Jack held Hassan's gaze; the striking blue eyes seemed incongruous in the tanned Arabic face. 'If your sons are dead then I am sorry for your loss, but we never killed anyone that wasn't trying to kill us. If events had been different we would be dead and your sons would be sitting here.'

'Perhaps, but that is not the case, Jack. May I call you, Jack?'

'You can call me what you like. I'm your prisoner.'

'You should think of yourself as our guest for the moment. How are your injuries?'

'I'll live.'

'Let's hope so, Jack. The ransom is due tomorrow at noon. I hope Dimitri Orlov is smart enough to pay for your release.'

'Me too!' said Jack, with a slight grin.

'All this could have been avoided if you and the rest of the western nations had stayed out of our affairs. You think you are the new crusaders, here to solve the problems of the Middle East. But you have no idea what is happening here. The seeds of the 'Arab Spring' have been sown; and soon it will become a raging fire that will burn through the oppressed nations being run by dictators and western puppets. Those nations will succumb to devastation. The people of those nations will rise and cry out for a strong Muslim ruler, a Caliph that will rid us of this foreign controlling pestilence and return us to the true Muslim faith.'

'Wow, you sound like you actually believe that. But this 'Arab Spring' you speak of; I have no idea what that is. But I do know the true Muslim faith is one of peace and love for your fellow man, I don't see much of that from you and your friends. You liken us to crusaders; well that's something I would never consider myself to be.'

'Yes, yes, crusaders, perhaps you think you are Richard the Lionheart?' snarled Hassan.

Jack stood up, holding his aching ribs and said, 'is there anything you want to actually discus, or do you just need me here as an audience for your ego?'

'Hrrrm... you are either very brave or very foolish. But we will talk again, Jack Castle.' Hassan stood and waved to the guard to take Jack back to his cell. Jack looked into the striking blue eyes again, turned and walked to the door. Before he left the room he looked back and said, 'I am definitely not Richard the Lionheart, and you, sir are certainly not Saladin.'

Chapter Thirteen
'Bedouin or Bandits'

The day in the desert had passed without incident and everyone managed sleep this time, even the camels were quiet; clearly the dunes had taken it out of men and beasts. By late afternoon the temperature had started to drop and the sun was an hour from setting. Tom had walked up to the top of the dune and was sitting looking out over the vast expanse of desert in front of him, *tough going*, he thought to himself, *probably not as tough as what Jack's putting up with though.*

He stood up and was about to go back down the dune, when movement in the far distance caught his peripheral vision. He watched for a few moments to be sure it was not his eyes playing tricks and then shouted, 'Sarmad, can you bring up the binoculars please?'

'What's the problem?' said Sarmad as he handed over the field glasses.

From the top of the dune Tom could see the dust cloud was getting bigger and closer. He passed the binoculars to Sarmad and said, 'What'd you think that is?'

After studying the cloud for a few moment he said, 'Looks like nine or ten men, maybe more, on horseback. Most likely Bedouin, moving to the north east of us.'

'You think it's a problem?' said Tom.

'They may come this way if they see us, but there's no reason to expect them to do that if they are Bedouin.

'And if they're not?'

'Then they could be bandits.'

Tom took the field glasses and looked at the cloud again, 'Hrrm, okay, let's get back down to the guys.'

When he saw the look on Tom's face, Ian said, 'What's the problem, boss?'

'A column of riders, out to the north of us,' then passing the binoculars to Ian, Tom continued, 'Sarmad reckons they could be Bedouin.'

Ian raised the powerful field glasses to his face and after a few seconds said, 'I dinnae think they're heedin north anymore.'

'And if they aren't Bedouin?' said Danny.

'They could be bandits,' answered Sarmad.

The cloud was clearly visible to the naked eye when Sarmad said, 'They are definitely coming this way.'

'Okay, we assume they are a threat, so we prepare accordingly, but if they pass us by peacefully, then we let them go. Agreed? ' said Tom.

The group nodded as Kevin said, 'So what's the plan, boss?'

'Sarmad, how about some local knowledge please?' said Tom.

Everyone looked at Sarmad, as the cloud in the distance, grew bigger.

'If they dismount and come towards us in single file, then they mean to greet us and pass us by,' explained Sarmad.

'And if not?' said Santosh and Danny in unison.

'If they intend to attack us, they will stay mounted and come towards us spread out. The leader out front will check us over first. He will be pleasant and greet us normally. But if he removes the cloth from his face and mouth and then turns to smile at his men.'

'What?' said Danny with obvious impatience.'

'Then they mean business, my friend!'

Tom took the glasses and looked at the approaching column. 'They look to have AK47's and shotguns.'

As he picked up his Mac10 machine pistol, Danny said, 'At short range an AK's no match for this baby.'

'How'd you want to play it, Tom?' said Steve.

Tom considered the terrain for a few seconds then said, 'Steve, take the sniper rifle and your Mac to the top of the dune. If the leader does his thing with the facecloth, you take him out and then come down the hill and concentrate on the group's right flank.'

Steve nodded, picked up his own weapon and the rifle case and made his way up the   side of the steep dune.

'Danny, you and Kev, take the left flank, get a position over there, cover yourselves with a pile of camel blankets and stay out of sight until it kicks off.'

'Sarmad, Santosh, you're with me upfront, okay?'

'Ian, take the right flank and support Steve when he comes down the hill.'

After checking weapons and ammunition, the group moved quickly into position and waited the arrival of the oncoming horsemen.

Tom, Sarmad and Santosh stood facing the oncoming column, each concealing their weapons under their riding robes. Ian was several yards to the right, weapon concealed; safety-catch off.

The bandits were fifty yards away when they changed from moving in single file to a spread out group.

'Oh shit,' said Santosh.

'Be cool,' said Tom, as he raised his hands in greeting.

The bandits stopped ten yards in front of the small encampment and the leader moved forward a couple of paces. He had an AK47 across his saddle, and a curved sword hanging from his belt. His robes were deep blue and covered in dust. His head was wrapped in the same cloth as his robes and his nose and mouth were obscured by the face-cloth. Only his eyes were visible. Tom watched as the man looked at the camels and equipment.

'Salaam Alaikum,' he said.

'Alaikum Salaam,' replied Sarmad, as he raised his hand and then held it over his heart in salute, 'you are most welcome to join us for food and drink, brother,' Sarmad continued.

From the corner of his eye, Tom could just make-out the muzzle of Steve's rifle on top of the dune and for a second felt somewhat safer.

'You have a lot of animals for such a small party,' continued the bandit boss, 'and you travel with foreigners.'

'Tell him we are an expedition from the World Health Organisation,' said Tom.

The leader nodded slowly, then raised his left hand to his face, rubbed his nose and then slowly removed the facecloth. He smiled, revealing a row of discoloured, broken and missing teeth.

As he turned his head, the bullet from Steve's high powered rife went through his neck and into the abdomen of the bandit next to him. Tom, Sarmad and Santosh swiftly opened up with their Mac10's, as the closest bandit fired his shotgun at them. Santosh went down with the full blast of the shotgun to his chest, knocking him back several feet. Ian was spraying the right flank of the group as Steve appeared from the top of the dune firing into the bandits as he ran down the hillside. The horses reared as the firefight began and two of the men were unseated, one being trampled by his own horse. Kevin and Danny strafed the left flank as twelve-hundred rounds a minute spewed from their automatic weapons.

From start to finish, the action had taken only twelve seconds. The bandits really never stood a chance, all nine were dead. Three horses were dead and one wounded and bellowing in distress was put out of its misery by Steve; the rest had bolted. Ian was at Santosh's side checking his carotid when the Indian groaned and opened his eyes.

'You okay, big man?' said Ian.

'Yeah, yeah,' he said, as he sat up. Then, ripping open the shredded robes, revealed his body armour and said, 'God bless, Kevlar.'

'Aye,' said Ian, 'but if the shot had bin a wee bit higher, ye'd be telling him that yerself.'

The firefight with the bandits had heightened everyone's awareness and appreciation of what they had to do. In a way, Tom was secretly pleased, as the incident proved to him that his band of friends was still a cohesive, viable and formidable force. Steve was riding alongside him and he said. 'What you thinking about, mate?'

'The bandits,' said Tom, 'our guys did well.'

'Of course we did,' said Steve smiling.

After four hours of steady riding, the caravan stopped to rest the animals and check their position.

'A wee bit over thirty-five miles tae the ootskirts o' the toon,' said Ian.

Looking at Sarmad, Tom said, 'Okay, good. So if we rest for an hour and then push hard, we should be there about o-two-hundred hours?'

'About two o clock in the morning, yes, boss,' confirmed Sarmad, 'that'll give me enough time to get down to the bridge, set the explosive charges and be back by o-three-hundred.'

'So we assault the compound between three and four o-clock. Let's hope they're all asleep,' added Tom.

'If they're not, they will be, once we give em a whiff of the Russian gas.' said Dan.

The group laughed and then Steve said, 'they will indeed mate. Just don't forget to put your bloody gas mask on before you use the stuff.'

Chapter Fourteen
'Al Raqqah'

It was just before two in the morning, as they stood on the wide plateau looking out over the city of Al Raqqah. The kidnapper's compound was one of several agricultural developments spread out along the southern edge of the city and about three miles from their current position. From their hilltop viewpoint and with the light of an almost full moon, they could see the whole of Raqqah. The Euphrates River to the south meandered its way east and shimmered in the moonlight, on its journey to Iraq. At the foot of the steep hill was a deserted shepherds hut and stable. The once straw roof of the stable had gone, but the hut was in reasonable condition for the group to unload all equipment and check weapons.

'We'll leave the camels here,' said Sarmad.

'Okay, agreed,' said Tom, then looking at his watch, 'time for you to get down to the bridge, Sarmad.'

Taking the plastic explosive and the detonators, he said, 'What time do we want the charges to go off?'

'It's just after two now,' said Tom, 'how long for you to get to the bridge, set the charges and get back here?'

'I'll take one of the animals and go straight to the river. Then move along the bank to the bridge, no more than thirty minutes. Ten minutes to set the charges and thirty minutes back.'

'Right, so you should be back here by o-three-fifteen. We move down to the compound on foot; with a fast pace, we should be there in twenty minutes from here. Assess and neutralise any guards. Zap the building with the gas then locate Jack and The Fox. We should be clear on our way by o-four-hundred. So that's your detonation time, set to blow the bridge at four.'

Sarmad nodded and smiled, 'Four o-clock, inshallah.'

'Inshallah,' said Tom as he shook Sarmad's hand, 'good luck. Be safe.'

The group watched as their friend climbed onto the grumbling camel and trotted off towards the Euphrates.

'When that bridge blows it's gonna wake the whole bloody town,' said Danny.

'That's the plan,' said Tom with a grin, 'and hopefully they'll think we escaped across the river and they'll be looking for us in that direction.'

The next hour was spent cleaning and checking weapons and equipment. Ian had confirmed Jack's exact location in the compound to within two meters. Opposition numbers though, was anyone's guess. Surplus water and food supplies had been concealed in the shepherd's hut, as well as the weapons that had been taken from the Bedouin bandits. On Sarmad's safe return, there was a final weapons and equipment check.

'Everybody good to go?' said Tom.

Affirming nods and thumbs-up from the group, followed by a, 'Let's rock 'n'roll' from Danny.

With Sarmad and Tom on point and Danny and Steve at the rear, the team began a steady jog towards the sleeping city.

Chapter Fifteen
'The Compound'

A wide drainage gully, running from the city to the river, provided cover for the team to assess the situation. The moon illuminated the surrounding area and with the exception of a few wondering goats, nothing moved. In the moonlight a small community mosque could be seen about a hundred and twenty yards to the east of the compound. Tom moved closer to Steve and whispered, 'You and Danny get over to that mosque. If you can get in and up the minaret, you should be able reconnoitre the inside of the compound with the night scope. Get back here as fast as you can.'

Steve nodded, and then tapped Danny on the shoulder. Without a word the two friends moved silently along the drainage ditch and out towards the tiny mosque.

From the top of the minaret and with the powerful night scope, Steve could see clearly over the wall and into the compound. A single storey farmhouse building was typical of the region. Two smaller outhouses stood away from the main building with a large canvas covered area against the north wall; he could see the back end of a large 4x4 protruding from beneath the canvas. Something caught his eye and he raised his head, blinked a couple of times then looked into the night scope again. There it was again, a tiny glow from a cigarette. *At least one guard patrolling the interior,* he thought.

Danny was waiting outside. 'Okay?' he whispered as Steve came out.

'Yeah, it's cool,' he replied quietly, 'let's go.'

Back at the drainage ditch Steve quickly explained the layout of the interior to the group. With the exception of the canvased area it was the same as the satellite pictures the CIA had provided.

'It's a covered parking place; so they have vehicles. That makes it easier.' said Tom.

'I could make out at least one big four-by-four, but there could be more,' said Steve.

'Okay, gentlemen,' continued Tom, 'one more time. Steve, Danny, Kev, you guys will locate and secure The Fox. Secondary objective is to recover any treasure.'

'Treasure?' said Danny.

'Treasure is what spooks call high value intelligence; we need to recover any documents, laptops, anything that may be of value,' explained Steve.

'Correct,' said Tom, 'but only if the opportunity presents itself, the man is the prime target. Any questions?'

'What if they start coming round before we find the guy?' said Kev.

'Silenced weapons or knives only, do not go 'loud' unless we absolutely have to. We've no idea how many we're up against, stealth is our strongest weapon.'

'Roger that, boss,' said Kev.

'Ian, you're with me. If Jack's hurt, or if the gas affects him adversely, he'll need your help.'

'Okay, Tom.'

'And most importantly, Sarmad, Santosh, you need to secure transport. If we have no way of escape, all else is worthless. I'm sure you guys can acquire something suitable,' he said with a grin, 'we'll need at least two vehicles, three would be better.'

'Anything but bloody camels!' said Danny.

Chapter Sixteen
'The Farmhouse'

A rusty old oil-drum provided a convenient, though unstable platform for Tom to look over the perimeter wall. There were no lights, other than one at the door of the farmhouse, but the moon provided sufficient illumination for him to see. In the far corner of the compound he saw a small puff of smoke and the glow from the guard's cigarette. Raising the sniper rifle to his shoulder and resting the muzzle on the wall, he waited for the kidnapper to draw on the cigarette again. The tiny bright red end of the cigarette glowed as the man inhaled. The high velocity bullet went straight through his nose and out the back of his skull. He fell to the ground with a dull thud and Tom waited to see if anyone responded to the noise, but only the sound of the goats down by the gully could be heard. He looked through the night scope at the prone body of the guard and said quietly to himself, 'Smoking will kill ya!'

Getting carefully down from the oil-drum, he said, Okay, Santosh, over you go, buddy. Get the gates open.'

The big Santosh smile appeared as he climbed onto the drum. Silently he slipped over the wall and dropped effortlessly down the other side. Tom quickly joined the rest of the team at the front gate and waited impatiently for the Indian to let them in.

The hinges on the big old gate creaked, so Santosh only opened a gap wide enough for everyone to slip through.

Tom nodded and Sarmad moved forward to join Santosh. Tom patted them each on the shoulder then gave a thumbs-up, as they slipped away towards the parking area.

The single storey farmhouse appeared to be constructed in two parts. An original older, somewhat rundown structure, with a smaller, more recent extension added to the side elevation. The main double doors were closed, with the dim light over the entrance. The windows were covered by dry and cracked wooden shutters.

The group split into their teams and spread out around the building. After securing gas masks over their faces, they unclipped the KO1 from their belts and carefully removed the safety pins. The shuttered windows made it easy to pump in the gas and within less than two minutes they were all back at the main door.

Cautiously entering the building, Tom immediately saw a prone figure at the side of the corridor; smiling to himself, he turned to Steve and gave a thumbs-up. The main corridor split into two smaller ones and Tom waved his left hand indicated the second team to move in that direction. Ian and Tom continued to the right and moving swiftly but silently, checked the doors on each side of the dimly lit hallway.

At the parking area, Sarmad and Santosh were surprised to find two dust covered Toyota Landcruisers and two double cab Toyota Pickups. One of the pickups had a filthy canvas tarpaulin cover, which Santosh quietly pulled back to reveal several fuel cans secured on the flat-back. He jumped up and quickly checked each can. 'These are all full,' he said smiling.

Sarmad grinned and nodded, then checked the first of the two Landcruisers. The key was in the ignition and after checking the rest of the vehicles found keys in them all. 'That's very kind of them to leave the keys, eh?'

'They must have been expecting us,' said Santosh with a grin.

'Let's hope not!' said Sarmad.

Back in the farmhouse, Steve's team proceeded as quickly as Tom's, checking every door, finding collapsed figures in almost every room. In one they were surprised to see a woman tied to the bed. She was unconscious, as was the man on the floor next to her. Her hijab had been removed from her head and her thick black hair hung over the side of the dirty mattress. Steve quickly entered the room and checked the woman's pulse.

'What the hell're you doing, Steve,' said Danny.

'These bastards have her prisoner for some reason. We're not leaving her. We'll come back for her once we find the target.'

Two more rooms revealed more of the hapless enemy and then, at the end of the hallway they found a more robust door that gave access to the extended part of the farmhouse.

'It's locked,' said Danny, after trying the handle.

'Stand back,' said Steve as he kicked the solid wood. The door rattled loudly, but did not give way.

'Okay, both of us,' he said to Dan.

The two men charged the door and it broke away at its hinges. Kevin rushed in to cover them, but no threat presented itself. The room was lit by two small lamps. On the floor and slumped against the wall was a man with a grey straggly beard and long grey hair. He wore a brown cotton robe with a thick knotted rope loosely around his waist. He was surrounded by several books and papers and in front of him was an open laptop.

'Kev, watch the door.' said Steve, 'this looks like our guy.'

Steve moved the man's head. The lower part of the right ear was missing and the cluster of scars on his neck was white against his dark skin. To be sure, he looked at the right hand and the little finger was gone.

'Is it him?' said Dan, impatiently.

'Yeah. Collect all these books and the laptop, Danny.'

Steve pulled the man to his feet and realised how tall he was, but he was slim, so it was an easy task to manhandle him over his shoulder.

'Can you manage?' said Kevin.

'Yeah, I got him. You got everything we need, Danny?'

'Good to go.'

'Kevin quickly led the way back along the dim corridor and stopped at the room with the woman. 'You sure we need to take her?'

'Pick her up, Kev and let's get the fuck out.' said Steve.

In the older part of the building Tom said, 'this could be it,' then, looking through the small barred opening in the middle of the door continued, 'yeah this is it.'

Slipping the two bolts, the door swung opening easily on its big hinges. The figure lying in the corner was as unconscious as the rest of the inhabitants in the farmhouse.

'It's him,' said Tom, seeing the bandaged hand.

Ian rolled Jack over carefully and checked his pulse, then gave a thumbs-up, saying, 'let's get him out.'

They manhandled him to a standing position, then with Jack in between; each took an arm and supported him over their shoulders. His dead-weight was not easy to contend with, but they dragged him from the cell and out into the corridor. Within a few seconds they were out of the building and into the courtyard. Jack was laid on the ground and Ian immediately administered the oxygen.

'Steve, comeback,' said Tom into his throat mic.

'Go ahead, Tom.'

'Steve, we have him, we're outside.'

'Roger, that. We got our man. On our way.'

Ian was still administering oxygen as Tom said, 'how is he?'

'I can't see a fucking thing,' said Jack, as he rubbed his eyes.

'Dinnae rub yer eyes, boss. Just keep blinking, yer sight'll come back in a wee minute.'

Tom knelt at his friend's side and grasped his hand, 'good to see you, Jack.'

Santosh had appeared and said, 'How's the boss?'

Grinning, Jack said, 'that you, Santosh?'

Before he could answer the second team came through the open door of the farmhouse.

Tom stood and lifted The Fox's head to look at his face. 'So this is the big-man?'

'That's him,' said Steve, 'gimme a hand Santosh.'

Jack was sitting now and said, 'help me up.'

Seeing the second figure across Kevin's shoulder, Tom said, 'who the hell's this?'

'These bastards had her prisoner, Steve wanted her freed.'

Tom nodded, 'Okay,' then turned to Santosh, 'transport?'

'Four vehicles, this way.'

'Right, guys, let's move.' said Tom.

Chapter Seventeen
'Boom'

Tom helped Jack into the passenger seat of the first Landcruiser, then said, 'Kev, put her in the back. Steve, Danny, you two in the other Landcruiser with, him. And get some cable-ties on his hands before he comes round.'

Danny opened the door and Steve flipped the unconscious man onto the back seat, bumping the man's head on the door opening in the process. 'Oh, sorry, mate!' said Steve with a grin; then taking a thick nylon cable-tie secured the man's hands.

Santosh and Ian had climbed into the first pickup and Kevin and Sarmad into the last vehicle. The engines all kicked into life and Tom backed out and into the centre of the compound. 'How you feeling, mate?'

'Sight's still a bit blurry and my head is fucking splitting, but other than that. I'm great and very pleased to see you, buddy.'

The rest of the small convoy had formed up and they moved swiftly towards the main gates. Leaving enough space, Tom stopped and dismounted; then quickly pulled each heavy door wide open, to the accompaniment of screeching hinges. Back in the driver's seat he gunned the powerful engine and the Landcruiser accelerated away from the compound with the other three vehicles close behind. Within five minutes they were away from the farming suburbs and into the countryside. They pulled off the road and parked up behind a small clump of olive trees. The woman was still unconscious on the back seat, but Jack had regained his sight and looking at her said, 'It's the doctor.'

Tom was out of the vehicle and had opened the rear door to check her pulse when Ian came up to him. 'I've just checked the big man and he's still oot cold. His breethin is a wee bit shallow, but the old guy's okay. How's this one?'

The rest of the team had congregated around the lead vehicle, all eagerly wanting to speak to Jack. Santosh handed him a can of Red Bull, saying, 'Here you go, boss.'

Jack smiled, took the can and after opening it drank the lot, smiled again and said. 'I really needed that.'

Steve, grinning, gave Jack a bear-hug which made him wince, 'Oh, sorry, boss,'

'It's okay, mate, still got a few bruised ribs,' said Jack.

Kevin, shook hands saying, 'Good to see you in one piece, boss, really good to see you.'

Danny and Sarmad were both looking towards the south, when Jack said, 'Nice to see you two as well?'

'Hold on, boss, any minute now,' said Dan.

The words were hardly out of Danny's mouth when the flash of the huge explosion lit up the horizon, south of the city. The shock wave reverberated through the calm night air as Sarmad's charges destroyed the main bridge across the Euphrates.

'That should wake the city,' said Sarmad, then turning to Jack continued, 'Salaam Alaikum, sidi, good to see you again my friend.'

'Salam, Sarmad, I'm very happy to see you too,' replied Jack, with a grin.

Danny came over and embraced Jack, 'Great t'see you in one piece, boss.'

'Right gentlemen, we need to move. Let's get to the pick-up point and signal the choppers,' said Tom.

As they mounted their respective vehicles, they saw lights coming on all over the city.

Another ten minutes driving and they were back at the old shepherds hut. The camels bellowed and snorted, as the arrival of the vehicles disturbed their sleep.

Ian took the navigation equipment and made his way up the steep banking to the plateau above. He set up the gear and took an accurate GPS position. Once he was satisfied the co-ordinates were one hundred percent correct, he sent a hi speed signal to Erbil. Within twenty seconds he received confirmation of his signal, plus the code-word indicating the choppers were on their way.

At the foot of the hill Steve and Danny waited patiently for The Fox to come-round. Kevin, Santosh and Sarmad made cursory checks of the vehicles and fuel; even though they were to be airlifted out, they could still have to move if the situation arose.

'So who is she?' said Tom.

'She's a doctor, her name's Mina Siddiqi. They brought her in to check me over a couple'o days ago. She was kind.'

'They had her prisoner,' said Tom, 'Steve said she was tied to a bed.'

'I hope they didn't abuse her,' said Jack, as the prone doctor groaned and said, 'They didn't, but I think the man in the room with me, intended too. So your rescue was timely.'

As she tried to sit up, Jack moved in and helped her, as he stopped her rubbing her eyes he said, 'Just blink hard, don't rub. The sight loss will be gone in a few minutes, its after effects of the knock-out gas.'

'Ahh, okay, I understand. Is that you, Jack?'

'Yes, it's me, you're safe now.'

'May I have some water please?'

Steve arrived at the vehicle and seeing the doctor had come round, said, 'How's she doin?'

'She'll be fine, thanks to you,' said Tom.

She stopped blinking and said, 'I can see now, still a little hazy but clearing. Someone said thanks to you?'

'I'm Tom and this is Steve. His team found you and brought you out.'

'I carried you out,' said Kev, as he joined the little group, 'my name is, Kevin.'

'Then I must thank you all, gentlemen. I'm not sure why they imprisoned me?'

'Probably because you knew I was there. They might have let you go after they'd finished with me, but who knows?' said Jack.

'You're free now anyway,' said Steve, 'how're you feeling?'

'Fine. A hell of a headache, but fine.'

'Hey!' shouted Danny, 'he's coming round.'

'Stay here, doc.' said Jack.

The focus of the group turned to the man in the second Landcruiser. 'So you're the famous, Fox?' said Danny.

* * *

100

Qassim Nasari had been tending goats since he was seven years old. He was now eleven and had been the main breadwinner for his family since his father had been taken by the regime. He lived in a small house on the edge of the city, with his mother and younger brother. Theirs was a poor existence, but they did have a small herd of goats that continued to breed and produce reasonable amounts of milk. The sale of a slaughtered goat provided occasional income as well as a food source for the family and the surplus milk was sold to the farming community along the southern edge of the city.

The top of the old olive tree gave a good vantage point for Qassim to sit and watch over his small herd of animals. He'd been half asleep when he was disturbed by the arrival of several men, dressed in black and with many guns. The men had waited in the drainage ditch and then later had disappeared into the nearest compound. Many minutes later, he saw the gates of the compound open and four trucks drive out and away towards the plateau, east of the city. The nocturnal goings on did not concern him and he continued to watch over his precious goats from his treetop position. He was almost asleep again when the sound of a huge explosion caused him to fall from the tree and the herd to scatter.

Chapter Eighteen
'You Stink'

Ian came down from the plateau and said, 'Sent oor position tae the choppers, they should be here in aboot an oor and fifteen minutes.'

'Well done, Ian,' said Tom

'Yeah, we just need to sit tight now,' added Jack, 'in the meantime can you check the old guy over, please?'

'Aye, nae bother, boss. We dinnae want him pegging oot on us, afore we hand him over do we?' said Ian with a grin

The vehicles had been moved out of sight, at the rear of the small clump of buildings. The camels had been released and with a hefty slap to each of their rumps, from Sarmad and Santosh they trotted off towards the river. Tom and Jack had gone to the top of the hill and with high powered field-glasses could see headlights from several vehicles arriving at the compound. Looks like the boys in the farmhouse have all woken up and called in reinforcements,' said Jack.

'Any idea how many were holding you?'

'I only saw a couple but there was obviously a lot more as the place was pretty noisy most of the time,' answered Jack.

'We saw men in almost every room, while searching for you. So I reckon there could be twenty to thirty guys down there.'

'Plus the ones arriving now with vehicles,' said Jack.

'Yeah, let's hope they fall for the decoy and head south to look for us,' said Tom grinning.

'If they do, the old road bridge is about ten miles west of the one we blew,' said Jack, 'so it'll take them a good twenty minutes to get there; then head south to try and pick up signs of us. By the time they realise we didn't go south, it's gonna be another hour before they come back and figure we headed east to Iraq.'

'Yes, but by then we should be in the air and outta here.' said Tom, smiling.

'ETA for the choppers is about an hour now,' said Jack, 'let's get everyone up here.'

Tom held his throat mic and said, 'Steve, come back.'

'Tom, go ahead.'

'Steve, move everyone to the top of the hill please.'

'Roger that.'

A few minutes later, Tom and Jack watched as the group appeared from the shepherd's hut and began trudging up the steep incline.

It was still dark, but the moon gave light to the surrounding terrain and from their position on the plateau and with the help of the high powered field glasses, Jack watched as vehicles began arriving at the compound, 'Looks like those bastards are all awake and have called in reinforcements. Take a look.'

Tom took the binoculars and adjusted the focus, 'Yeah, there are quite a lot of vehicles arriving at the compound. They're gonna be well pissed off we snatched their top man,' said Tom grinning.

Steve helped the doctor up the steep incline. Santosh and Sarmad supported The Fox, who was finding it difficult to keep his balance due to the restraints on his hands; his breathing was laboured and he sat down a couple of times on the accent. Dan held his throat mic and said, 'Ian, come back.'

'Aye, Danny, go ahead.'

'The old man's struggling with his breathing. Can you bring the oxygen, please?'

'Aye, okay. B'right there.'

Several minutes later, Sarmad, Santosh and Ian appeared over the rim of the plateau, with the wheezing Fox between them.

'Is he okay?' said Jack.

'Aye, he's okay,' answered Ian, 'probably still sufferin a wee bit from the gas.'

'Good. We don't want him dying on us just yet,' said Jack.

'I have no intention of dying today, Jack Castle,' said The Fox.

Jack looked into the eyes of his former captor and even in the half-light of the moon saw the defiance in the old man, 'Ian, keep an eye on him till we get outta here,' said Jack.

Santosh dropped a large nylon bag on the ground and said with a huge grin,' Clean gear for you, boss. You should change, you bloody stink!'

Jack opened the bag and smiled, body armour, boots, black coverall, as well as underclothes and socks.

'Cheers, Santosh. Can you get me a few bottles of water as well please?' continued Jack, as he stripped off the filthy coverall.

'I'll check your hand as well,' said Mina.

After Jack had washed and changed into the clean clothes; the doctor redressed his bandaged hand, 'It's healed well, no infection,' she said.

Before he could answer, Tom said, 'Five vehicles leaving the compound. They are heading west, towards the old river bridge,' then handing the binoculars to Jack continued 'it looks like blowing the main bridge has done the trick. They've fallen for the decoy escape route and think we've gone south.'

Jack watched as the five vehicles disappeared along the river road, then walked over to Ian. 'How is he?'

'He's okay.'

Then, taking Ian away from the old man, asked quietly, 'How long till the choppers get here?'

Ian looked at his watch, 'ETA, aboot forty minutes, boss.'

* * *

There was panic and confusion in the farmhouse once the gas had worn off and the inhabitants had regained consciousness. The after effects were more disturbing, with most of the men thinking they were permanently blind and the rubbing of eyes only prolonged their recovery. It all added to the time the rescuers had to make good their escape. It was not long however until some sort of control was reinstated within the band of terrorists. Their panic returned when they discovered not only had their captive escaped, but their top man, their sheik, had been taken as well.

Walid Mansoori was the captain in charge of the team that had brought The Fox from Damascus to Al Raqqah and he alone was responsible for the sheik's safety. He had ordered the immediate and thorough search of the farmhouse and compound, but it was not long until it became clear whoever had rescued the infidel, and taken the sheik had Mansoori's own vehicles to make good their escape.

He instructed his subordinates to muster all other ISIL personnel from across the city and then went into his room alone. He looked at his reflection in the dirty cracked mirror. His eyes were still stinging, so he carefully rinsed his face and soothed the eyes with cool bottled water. After drying his face, he took out his cellphone and cleared his throat and took a deep breath. He pressed the speed dial and a few seconds later heard, 'Salam Alaikum.'

'Alaikum Salam, sidi. This is Captain Mansoori.'

'Yes, Mansoori, why do you call me on this secure number and at this hour of the day?'

'We have been attacked, sidi. They have taken the infidel.'

'Attacked? By whom? The Americans?'

'I do not know, sidi. They used a gas to knock us all out.'

'So you were overcome by someone you do not know and who rescued the infidel while you slept?'

'Yes, sidi. I am sorry, sidi, but there is more.'

'What more could there be Mansoori? You have made a grave mistake in not securing your prisoner.'

'Sidi, there is more.'

'Go on.'

He cleared his throat and took a deep breath. 'They have taken Sheik Hassan al Hamady.'

The line went quiet for several seconds, and then Mansoori said, 'Are you still there, sidi?'

'I am here,' there was a further pause and then, 'you must find the people who took Sheik Hassan, you must find them now. He cannot be taken captive alive. Do you understand me, Mansoori?'

'Yes, sidi, I will find him.'

'Do you understand me Mansoori? He cannot be taken captive alive!'

The line went dead.

Chapter Nineteen
'The Goatherd'

It was almost five-o-clock, with the sun still below the horizon, when Qassim Nasari walked into the compound with his two cans of goat's milk. The young goat-heard was surprised to see so many people milling around the yard. Usually there were half a dozen men and the two cans of milk he brought each day were enough. He smiled to himself at the thought of providing a lot more milk today.

'What the hell do you want? Get out!' shouted one of the men.

'Salaam, sidi,' said Qassim, unafraid and standing his ground. 'I bring the milk,' then holding up the cans continued, 'I bring the milk each day.'

Another man came from the farmhouse, one that Qassim recognised, 'Sidi, I bring the milk,' shouted Qassim, not wanting to lose the sale.

'Bring it in, little one,' said the familiar man.

With a smile on his dirty face, Qassim ran to the house and pushed passed the throng of men at the door.

'Excuse me, sidi, I must deliver my milk and get my money,' he said as he passed by the big man in the corridor.

Walid Mansoori, looked at the boy and said, 'Who are you, little brother?'

Qassim stood to his full three feet eight inches height and said with authority and pride, 'I am Qassim, the goatherd!'

'And where do you tend your goats, Qassim?' said Mansoori.

'Sometimes near the river, sidi, sometimes outside,' the little boy made a gesture with his hand, 'but most of the time outside near the olive trees and the drainage ditch.'

'It is early morning, have you been tending all night?'

'Yes, sidi, I guard my herd at night,' he took out a homemade catapult from a cloth bag at his waist and pulled it in a demonstration of his skill. 'And in the day time I go to school.'

'So little one, you were near our compound tonight?'

'Yes, sidi.'

'Did you see anything unusual this night, Qassim?'

'Yes, Sidi, many unusual things this night.'

Walid Mansoori smiled at the young boy, placed his hand on his shoulder and said, 'Come in here, Qassim. Bring your milk and tell me of the unusual things you saw.'

* * *

The mood on the plateau was bullish. The cool night air was warming up with the coming dawn and the sun would break over the horizon in the next half hour.

'Ian?' said Jack, 'ETA on the choppers, buddy?'

'Aboot twenty five minutes, boss. Maybe able tae get em on the radio the noo.'

'No. Just leave it for now. No need to give our location away until they are five minutes out,' replied Jack.

'Aye okay, boss.'

'Jack, Tom, you'd better take a look at this,' shouted Steve.

'Whatsup?' said Tom.

Steve handed him the binoculars and said, 'Check out those trucks.'

'What is it?' said Jack.

'It's fucking trouble, that's what it is, big fucking trouble.'

Jack took the field-glasses, 'Four vehicles and they are heading directly towards us.'

'Looks like they know where we are,' said Tom.

'How'd they know that?' said Steve.

'It doesn't matter how they know,' said Jack, 'but they'll be here in the next ten minutes.'

Chapter Twenty
'Rourke's Drift'

The group stood at the edge of the plateau and watched the headlights of the four vehicles getting closer.

'Okay, gentlemen, we have a couple of options,' said Jack, 'we can get down to the vehicles and make a run for the Iraqi border using the main road. If we do that we are sure to meet resistance on the way.'

'Next option, boss?' said Kevin.

'We use the vehicles and try and cross the desert,' said Jack.

'Vehicles cannot cross desert, sidi,' said Sarmad, 'some areas are okay, but camel or horse is the only way to cross safely.'

'Next option, boss?' said Kevin again.

'We make a stand here til the choppers arrive. We're in a good position. The incline is too steep for vehicles. They'd have to get up on foot and we have the advantage of a superior position.'

'They could drive to the end of the plateau and flank us,' said Danny.

'Yeah,' said Tom, 'but the choppers'll be here before they could do that.'

'So we make a stand here?' said Steve.

'Rourke's Drift all over again,' grinned Danny.

'I bloody hope not!' added Kevin.

'Jack?' said Tom.

Jack knelt down and began drawing in the sand, 'Okay, guys, this is the plan. Tom, Ian, Sarmad, you'll stay up here. Sarmad, stick with the old man, if it all goes wrong and we are over run, he must not be allowed to be rescued alive.'

'Yes, sidi, I understand.'

'Tom, you cover us with the sniper rifle, you're the best marksman, take out as many of them as you can before they get too close. Steve, you cover from here as well and support Tom. Ian, get on to the choppers, our position's blown now, so no need for radio silence. Let them know we need immediate support and extraction.'

'Aye, boss.'

Jack looked at the rest of the team and said with a grin, 'Now for the fun stuff. Danny, Kev, Santosh, you guys will come down to the shepherd's hut with me. We plant charges on the vehicle's fuel tanks. We take the spare fuel cans and conceal them at the bottom of the incline. I want remote detonators on all charges.'

'We should pick up the bandits AK47's and ammo,' said Kevin, 'the Mac10's are good for close quarters, but not much good over fifty yards.'

'What AK's? What bandits?' said Jack.

'Long story, no time now, tell you later,' said Danny grinning.

'Okay,' said Jack, 'any questions?'

'Rock 'n' roll,' said Danny.

The three men went over the edge of the plateau kicking up a small cloud of dust and sand as they ran down the steep incline. Before Jack left, he spoke quietly to Mina, 'Doc, you should go. Follow the plateau north. It looks like it runs out and down to ground level about a mile and a half from here. You could be back in the city in less than an hour.'

'I'll stay, Jack. I can help. Go, I'll see you soon.'

'Okay,' he said with a smile, 'no time to argue, see you soon.'

The sun was coming over the horizon and the plateau was bathed in the warm sunlight. The height of the plateau cast a long shadow to the west, so the oncoming vehicles were still in darkness. In the old hut it didn't take long for Kevin to quickly recover the six AK's and ammunition they'd taken from the desert bandits and within a few minutes he was heading back up the hill. At the rear of the ruined stable building Santosh had set charges on the two Landcruisers and the two pickups fuel tanks; while Jack and Danny had placed the spare fuel cans in two locations at the base of the incline. The three were half way up the hill when they heard the rapid fire from Tom's sniper rifle. Jack turned and saw the lead vehicle spin and roll over. The other vehicles reduced speed as each swerved to avoid hitting the stricken vehicle. Santosh was almost at the top of the hill, with Danny a few yards behind, but the pain in Jack's ribs had returned with the exertion and he was wheezing and coughing, as he fought to push on up the steep incline. There was another twenty yards to the top of the hill, when more shots from above rattled into the approaching vehicles below.

The terrorist vehicles screeched to a halt in a huge cloud of dust and sand, several yards from the foot of the incline. They stopped in an unorganised cluster and five or six men from each vehicle quickly dismounted and took cover behind their respective vehicles. It was difficult to see who, or how many were up on the plateau, but instinctively the terrorists all opened fire at the now sunlit ridge, just as Jack scrambled over the top.

'You okay, mate?' said Tom as he pulled his friend away from the edge.

'Jesus. I'm getting to old for this shit,' replied Jack with a grin.

Santosh was at his side and handed Jack a bottle of water, 'You okay, boss?'

'I am now!' said Jack as he swallowed half the contents.

The gunfire from below was having no effect on the team above; who had spread out and taken positions along the edge of the ridge. Santosh had the remote control for the charges and peered cautiously over the edge, waiting for the attackers to be in the optimum position. He looked across to Jack when he saw half a dozen men sprint across to the old shepherd's building and as Jack nodded, Santosh pressed the first remote, setting off the charges on the vehicles behind the tiny hut. The plastic explosive on the four fuel tanks went up with a huge fire ball and deafening explosion that reverberated up the escarpment and across the plateau. The hut and old stable building vanished and the stolen vehicles, became hundreds of huge chunks of flying shrapnel that killed several more of the startled attackers.

The explosion seemed to galvanise the attackers into action and several of them broke from the cover of their vehicles and ran towards the incline; indiscriminately firing their AK's at the ridge forty feet above. Jack and the rest of his friends conserved ammunition and took carful aim before returning fire. Their precise aim and the volley fire from the hilltop resulting in more attackers being taken out. The eight or so men who had broken cover were now at the base of the incline. Santosh waited a few seconds and then pressed the second remote. The two charges on the fuel cans went up each side of the hapless attackers. The men who weren't killed by the explosions were lost to the fireballs that ensued. Only a handful of terrorists now fired from the cover of their vehicles. The team on the hill top returned fire sporadically, but did not risk exposing themselves to the incessant gunfire from below.

'The choppers are here!' shouted Ian over the noise of the firefight.

Everyone to a man turned and saw the silhouettes of the two Blackhawks against the morning sun.

'You fucking beauty!' yelled Danny.

Ian moved away from the edge of the plateau, got on the radio and called the inbound helicopters, 'Maverick One, Maverick One, this is Bulldog.'

Jack and Tom moved away from the edge and joined Ian, 'Have you raised them, buddy?' said Jack, just as the radio squawked, 'Bulldog, Bulldog, this is Maverick One, we read you, loud and clear. We see your position directly in front of us. We are inbound, please advise situation.'

Ian passed the mic to Jack, 'Maverick One we are under fire from the base of the incline, multiple attackers. Can you support?'

'Bulldog, confirm your position with smoke please.'

Ian took a small canister from his body armour, tapped the end on the ground and threw it several yards from the group. Within a few seconds bright green smoke began to billow from the tiny canister.

'Bulldog, Bulldog, I have green smoke, confirm.'

'That's us, Maverick, green smoke confirmed,' said Jack.

'Roger that, Bulldog, keep your heads down, we're coming around now.'

Chapter Twenty One
'Blackhawk Down'

The two Blackhawks banked to the north and then swung around to follow the line of the plateau towards the attackers. The lead helicopter opened up with the under fuselage heavy machine gun, strafing the cluster of vehicles as it sped past. The side-door-gunner joined the attack as his weapon came into range. Hundreds of rounds of high velocity bullets ripped into men and vehicles as the second Blackhawk followed the first. As the choppers sped past and away to the south, the group of friends on the plateau stood and looked down at the devastation below. The remains of the first vehicles to be blown up still burned and sent a column of black acrid smoke into the still morning sky. The bodies of the men on the incline where strewn in grotesque positions, blooded and charred. The attacker's vehicles were riddled with heavy calibre bullet holes from the Blackhawks and the remaining attackers lay dead around their destroyed trucks.

The helicopters banked to the left and swung back towards the top of the plateau, 'Bulldog, Bulldog, this is Maverick One, stand-by, stand-by; coming in to land now.'

* * *

The lead vehicle, that Tom had taken out earlier, lay a hundred and fifty yards from the base of the escarpment.

The driver had been shot in the face and died instantly. The front seat passenger had taken two rounds in the chest and had died a few seconds later. The other two passengers in the rear had been hit as well. The vehicle had spun out of control with the death of the driver and after toppling over a couple of times, came to rest upside down on its roof.

Steam was still hissing from the fractured radiator, as a couple of large fragments of broken windscreen dropped from the frame with a clatter. The noise brought Walid Mansoori out of semi-consciousness. The man in the back seat next to him had been shot in the throat and was lying across his legs, blood covered Mansoori's trousers from his dead colleague, but the thick cloying blood on his shirt was from his own stomach. He felt his abdomen and winced at the immediate pain, *shot in the liver,* he thought to himself. With difficulty and the pain level rising, he managed to push the dead man from his legs and pull himself towards the smashed side window. Once out of the window he rested, his breathing shallow and laboured, the wound in his abdomen oozing black blood.

He heard no shooting, only the familiar sound of helicopter engines. He wiped the stinging sweat from his eyes and focussed on the scene of carnage before him; the black plume of smoke to the left, his own vehicles smoking, riddled with bullets, dead men, his men, scattered everywhere. He eased himself into a sitting position, gritting his teeth as the pain almost knocked him out again. He reached back into the vehicle to retrieve the AK47 of the man in the front seat and then saw the rocket grenade launcher under the man's twisted body.

* * *

The first Blackhawk came slowly into land, while the second helicopter hovered in a defensive position, a hundred yards away.

'Bulldog, Bulldog, Maverick One coming in to land now, our orders are to uplift the prime target and Maverick Two will extract your team. Over?'

'Maverick One, copy that. Prime target is in good condition and ready for extraction,' said Tom into the radio.

'Tom, it was your capture, you get the old guy ready and see him off, buddy,' said Jack.

Tom handed the shortwave radio to Jack and said, 'Steve, let's go.' as he walked over to the sitting figure of The Fox.

Steve took the old man's arm and helped him to his feet, 'Okay, matey you're outta here.'

The Fox looked Steve in his one good eye and then turned to the group watching, 'You are all dead men,' he shouted.

Tom took the old man's other arm and said, 'If I were you I'd be worrying more about myself than us, mate. You're probably on your way to sunny Cuba.'

The Fox looked at Tom, the crystal blue eyes defiant, 'I will never see Cuba.'

'Yeah, right,' said Steve, 'let's go.'

Maverick One had touched down in an unpleasant cloud of dust and sand that had covered the waiting group. Tom turned to Jack and nodded as he, Steve and the old man slowly walked with heads down, to the waiting helicopter. The pilot had disembarked and was waiting next to the open door. The side-door-gunner had his weapon trained on the approaching three men.

'Good morning, sir,' said the pilot as he extended his hand to Steve.

'Morning, Captain,' said Steve recognising the insignia on the pilots collar, 'I'm Steve, this is my boss, Tom.'

Tom shook hands with the young pilot, 'Good to see you, Captain, you were right on-time, sir. Thanks for your help.'

'Not a problem, Tom. This is our passenger?'

'Yessir,' said Steve, 'he's all yours.'

The captain gestured to the door gunner, who reached down and took hold of The Fox's upper arm and with the help of Steve and Tom pulled the old man through the open door. Tom watched as the gunner checked the restraints and then strapped him into a bulkhead seat.

'Okay, gentlemen, we'll get airborne. Your aircraft will be right here, as soon as we take up an over-watch position. We'll see you in Erbil,' said the pilot with a big smile.

'The beers will be on us,' said Steve, with an equally large grin.

Tom and Steve backed away from the Blackhawk as the rotors built up speed. The dust and sand was again kicked up as the big helicopter lifted off, hovered for a few seconds and then slowly climbed into the clear sky above the plateau.

* * *

Walid Mansoori had propped himself up against the side of the up-turned Landcruiser. His breathing was shallow and the blood from his abdomen had soaked his shirt and trousers. The sweat from his exertions stung his eyes and his lips tasted of salt as he tried to moisten then with his tongue. The rocket grenade launcher was heavy and he struggled to raise it to his shoulder, but the pain from his wound was too great. The noise of the helicopter's engines increased as it took off, and then it was there before him, high above the escarpment in clear view. He moaned in agony as he lifted the launcher onto the base of the up-tuned vehicle and flipped the safety catch to off. He took a deep breath and winced at the pain it caused, then after wiping the sweat from his eyes, he lined up the sights on the weapon and took careful aim. The helicopter hovered in the clear blue sky, waiting.

'Allah o Akbah,' he whispered with his dying breath and squeezed the trigger.

* * *

It was the door gunner who saw the rocket grenade approaching, 'RPG, RPG,' he yelled into the radio.

The pilot reacted as he'd been trained and muscle memory kicked in. He pulled on the cyclic control giving the helicopter height and pressed down hard on the right rudder pedal, turning the aircraft away from the approaching missile.

'Oh, fuck!' said Danny, as he dropped to the ground.

The rest of the group followed his lead and hit the deck instinctively, as the sound of the deadly projectile streaked towards the Blackhawk.

The pilot gripped the controls, willing his aircraft to respond and then the missile struck with a flash and an explosion that reverberated through the structure of the big helicopter. The control panel lit up with a dozen flashing warning lights and screeching alarms.

'Rear rotor's been hit,' shouted the pilot, as he fought to control the spin of his aircraft, 'no response from rudder control!'

'Mayday. Mayday. Mayday,' shouted the co-pilot into the radio.

Jack, Tom, and the rest of the group watched in silence, as the Blackhawk began to spin faster, smoke and flame billowing from the rear of the fuselage like breath from a dragon. On the stricken aircraft the pilot's fight with the controls was useless. Unable to bring the wounded Blackhawk under control, he shouted, 'We're going in!'

As if to confirm his words, the main rotors distorted under the strain, the nose dipped and the aircraft began to lose altitude.

'Mayday. Mayday. Mayday,' yelled the co-pilot, 'Maverick One, going in!'

As the helicopter spun faster, it increased its rate of descent and dropped below the plateau, veering towards the escarpment.

'Brace, Brace. Brace,' yelled the pilot, as the helicopter smashed into the steep hillside. The main rotors cut into the rock and sand and the doomed aircraft exploded in a huge crimson and gold fireball.

Chapter Twenty Two
'Stitched-Up'

Everyone in the Erbil Base control room listened to the last words of the pilot. His voice over the loud speaker filled the room and then nothing, only the crackle of static. A few seconds later the second pilot's voice came over the speaker, 'Echo Bravo, Maverick Two. Maverick One is down. I say again, Maverick One is down.'

'Maverick Two, this is Echo Bravo, report on survivors?'

'Echo Bravo, Maverick Two, no survivors, repeat, no survivors.'

Greg Stoneham, looked at Captain Charles Hamilton and said, 'Confirm prime target is still secured?'

'Maverick Two, confirm status of prime target?'

'Echo Bravo, Maverick Two, prime target is dead. We're going in now to extract the rescue team.'

Stoneham, moved to the radio operator and took the microphone, 'Maverick Two, this is Echo Bravo, negative on your last transmission. Pass them by.'

'Echo Bravo, repeat your last transmission please?'

'Maverick Two, your orders are to pass them by. This is a CIA operation, pass them by. Confirm understanding?'

'Echo Bravo, Maverick Two, understood. Returning to home base. Maverick Two, out.'

The small group on the top of the plateau watched as the Blackhawk turned away from their position. Jack spoke into the radio, 'Maverick Two, Maverick Two, this is Bulldog, we are ready for extraction, over.'

'Sorry, Bulldog, we have orders to return to home base. Good luck.'

'Maverick Two, we need immediate extraction, over. Maverick Two, come in please? Maverick Two?'

'What the fuck just happened?' said Danny.

'We just got fucked,' said Kevin.

Jack turned to Tom, raised his upturned palms in a gesture of incredulity, 'What the....?'

'CIA!' said Tom, before Jack could finish, 'they only wanted The Fox. He's dead and we don't count.'

'Wot a bunch o bastards,' said Ian.

'Some fucker's gonna pay for this,' said Steve.

'Yeah, they are, but right now we need to get the hell outta here,' said Jack, 'it won't be long until the bunch that went south looking for us will be back.'

'What's the plan, boss?' said Kevin.

'Let's move north down the plateau and find someplace to hold up, til we can figure a way out of this,' replied Jack.

'Okay, collect all weapons and ammo, water if there is any. Let's move,' said Tom

'We should gather the ammo from that bunch at the bottom of the hill,' said Steve.

'Good idea,' said Jack, 'Steve, Danny, Kevin, Santosh, you guys get down there and collect all the ammo you can, then catch up with us. Sarmad, look after the doctor please. Okay let's move.'

Sarmad moved alongside Mina and said, 'Just a second doc,' then removed the black and white cheque keffiyah from around his neck and handed it to Mina, 'This ok for your head, doctor?'

Taking the headscarf she smiled and said, 'Yes, thank you, Sarmad, you are very kind.'

As they walked, she deftly wrapped her hair into a knot and then covered her head and hair with the scarf. Sarmad smiled and nodded, then said 'It's ok?'

Mina returned the smile and the two increased their speed, to catch up with the rest of the group heading north along the wide plateau.

They had moved at a brisk walking pace until the four guys with the recovered ammo caught up, then the whole group broke into a steady jog. Steve and Danny on point, with Santosh and Kevin at the rear, they made good time moving further and further away from the top of the plateau. Jack looked back to see Mina, with Sarmad at her side, was keeping pace, despite her full length bourka flapping around her legs. The temperature was rising, but it was not too uncomfortable and they made swift progress. Within twenty minutes they were almost three miles away from the scene of the earlier incident and slowed the pace as they approached a large wild olive grove. The main group slowed to a walk, as Danny and Steve ran ahead to reconnoitre the clump of trees. A few moments later Jack saw Steve wave them forward. After everyone had gulped down some bottled water, they sat down in the shade and Jack said, 'Okay, let's reassess our situation.'

'We're in the shit,' said Danny.

'Errmm...yes, fraid so,' continued Jack, 'but let's think our way out of this eh?'

'We're not gonna get any help from the Yanks,' said Tom, 'we're on our own.'

'Maybe not,' said Jack, 'Ian, gimme the satellite phone please?'

Jack took the phone and stood up, checking signal strength on the small screen, once he had acquired the communications satellite he punched in a dozen numbers, then waited for several seconds for the connection to be made.

'Hello, Mathew Sterling.'

'Mathew, this is, Jack. What the hell is going on?'

'What do you mean?'

'Don't you know, Matt?'

'Just tell me what the hell you're on about, Jack. Aren't you on your way back?'

'Someone has left us out to dry, Mathew. Maverick One went down with The Fox on board and then Maverick Two said they had been ordered back to base. They left us out here.'

'Jack, are you and your guys safe?'

'We had contact with about thirty plus of the opposition, they were all taken out, we are all okay, but we're not in a good situation here. We need extraction with all haste, Matt.'

'Okay, let me go find Captain Hamilton, see what the hell is going on. Can you sit tight and call me back in fifteen minutes?'

'Will do. Just get us the hell outta here.'

'What's the score, boss?' asked Kevin.

'I've just spoken with Matt Sterling; he'd no idea we've been left in the shit. Oh, sorry, Mina, 'scuse my French.'

'What's he gonna dae aboot it?' said Ian.

'I'm calling him back in fifteen, let's stay cool. Check your weapons while we wait.'

Tom moved over to Jack and said quietly, 'What d'you think?'

Shaking his head, Jack answered in a hushed voice, 'We've been stitched up by the Yanks, no doubt about that, but why? Just need t'see what Matt comes back with.'

The fifteen minutes seemed endless and then Jack made the second satellite call.

'Jack? hi again. Okay it's all pretty weird here. I've spoken with Captain Hamilton and he was in the control room while the extraction was going on. Once Maverick One went down with the loss of the prime target, Gregg Stoneham gave the order for the second chopper to pass you by and return to base.'

'I don't understand?' said Jack frowning.

'Nor do I, Jack, and neither do the military here. Hamilton said Stoneham over-ruled him and called the play. Stoneham said it was a CIA operation and he gave the order to leave you guys.'

'Okay, well you can tell Mr Stoneham we will be talking to him when we get back.'

'Don't think so. He's gone, left the base. No one knows why or where he is.'

'Something stinks here,' said Jack, 'but he's not our concern for the moment. Can you get Hamilton to send the chopper back for us?'

'I've asked him but he's reluctant to do so. He's a career officer, not likely to risk anything for us. Tell him we have treasure. We have The Fox's laptop and several ledgers all of which will have valuable information.'

'Really? That didn't get put on the same chopper as The Fox?'

'We're not that naïve, Matt. The Yanks wanted the old man in return for providing support, but any intelligence we picked up was always going to be passed to you, buddy.'

'Same old Jack, always has a backup plan. Okay, I have an idea, but it'll take a little while to put it together. Give me an hour or so to make some calls?'

'Yes, sure, Matt, talk again in sixty minutes.'

Jack turned to the group, 'It was that bastard Stoneham. It was his call to leave us here once they lost The Fox. The CIA screwed us.'

'Okay, boss, so how do we get out of here now?' said Steve.

'I'm calling Mathew back in an hour. He's working on an extraction plan.'

'How the fuck do we know this guy is gonna help us?' said Danny.

'Yeah,' added Ian, 'we ken he's yur pal, boss. But how much can we trust a spook?'

'We can trust Mathew Sterling, guys.' said Tom.

'Why?' continued Danny,' we just got shafted by the CIA, why should we trust bloody MI6?'

Okay, okay,' said Jack, 'calm down and listen. I've known Mathew all my life. In his younger days he was gonna be a doctor, but circumstances changed and instead of going to Edinburgh he went to Cambridge and studied political science and eastern languages. MI6

129

recruited him directly from university and he's been with them ever since.'

'That still doesn't mean we can trust him, boss,' said Kevin.

Jack raised his hand and continued, 'Sterling is Matt's mother's maiden name. Sterling is my mother's maiden name. Mathew Sterling is my brother.'

Chapter Twenty Three
'Good News & Bad News'

It was late morning and the sun was high in the sky, when Jack made his third call to Mathew Sterling. The satellite phone rang once and the voice on the other end said, 'Jack?'

'Mathew, have we a plan?'

'Yes, we have, but there's good news and bad news!'

'Good news first please, Matt.'

'Okay, we've arranged for a Sea King helicopter to come from the British base at Akrotiri on Cyprus.'

'The Sea King is a search and rescue aircraft,' interrupted Jack.

'Exactly,' said Mathew, 'we can't send in a military aircraft, so this is the best we can come up with at short notice. However, there'll be a small group of 'professionals' on-board, should you need support at the extraction point.'

'Understood,' said Jack smiling. Okay, gimme the bad news.'

'Bad news is your gonna have to get across Syria's northern border and into Turkey.'

'We can do that. What's the deal?'

'There's no way we can fly into Syria, but the Turks have agreed to let us send the Sea King into their airspace for a limited time. We've advised them your team is a group of British aid workers who were attacked by ISIS and you need to be extracted with all haste.'

'Okay, go on.'

'Take down these co-ordinates.'

'Hold one please. Ian, note these co-ordinates. Okay go ahead, Matt.'

Slowly and clearly, Mathew said, 'Latitude, thirty-six degrees, forty-four minutes. Longitude thirty-nine degrees, thirteen minutes.'

Jack repeated the position to Ian and Ian read back the numbers, with Jack giving thumbs up by way of confirmation.

'What time is the rendezvous?' continued Jack.

'You must be at that location tomorrow morning at o-nine-hundred hours; it's a few miles south of a small town called Garac. Call sign for the chopper is Empire.'

'Roger that. We'll sort out transport and be there. Cheers, Mathew.'

'Okay, Jack, but don't be late, the chopper will only be on the ground for ten minutes and then it's gone.'

'Understood. Thanks again, Mathew.'

'I'll see you in Akrotiri, Jack. Good luck, be safe.'

Jack sat down and leaned against a thick trunked olive tree. Looking at each of his friends in turn he said, 'Good news and bad news, gentlemen.'

The group listened in silence until Jack had reiterated the extraction plan. No one spoke until Sarmad asked, 'Who are the small group of professionals, boss?'

'Military,' answered Jack, 'Royal Marines or maybe SAS, both regiments have personnel on Cyprus.'

'So how do we get across the border?' said Danny.

'Ian, how far to the border and the rendezvous point?'

'Wait a wee minute,' said Ian as he began checking the GPS.

'The border's aboot eighty miles, boss. The RV's another fifteen miles into Turkey, near a wee toon called Garac.'

'That's correct,' said Jack, 'Okay, the plan is evade and escape. We need to find a safe place to hold up and then secure transport across the northern border.'

'I can help with both of those.' said Mina.

Getting to her feet the doctor looked into the faces of this tough group of men. *Tough yet kind, yes kind,* she thought, *and they no doubt saved my life.*

'May I have some water please?' she said to Sarmad; who took out a small bottle from his back pack. After refreshing her throat she smiled and said, 'My father has several large farms to the north of the city. He also has many trucks which he uses to transport goods to and from Turkey. He will help you get out of Syria. If we can contact him, he will bring a truck here. Then take you north of the city, to one of the farms. Tomorrow he will take you to safety.'

The group looked at each other in silence and then Tom said, 'I guess we're all thinking, is this a safe option?'

'I'm thinking it might be our only option,' said Jack, 'and why shouldn't the doc's father help us? We helped her.'

'I agree,' said Steve, 'we pulled her out of there and god knows what would have happened to her if we hadn't. I think we go with the doc's dad.'

Jack looked out towards the city. The road, a mile away, which skirted Al Raqqah, was busy with trucks, cars and the odd government military vehicle. Then turning back to his friends he said, 'Ian, sat-phone please.'

As he handed over the phone, Ian said, 'Ye sure aboot this, boss?'

Nodding to Ian, Jack walked over to Mina. 'Tell him you are safe. Tell him you need to be picked up in a truck. Do not say why, but you need a truck not a car. Do not say anything about us. You need him here right away. Okay, doc?'

'I understand,' said Mina smiling, 'don't worry he will help. You will not be at risk.'

'Okay, what's the number?'

After punching the digits into the phone, Jack waited for several long seconds as the phone at the other end rang and rang. 'No answer?' he said.

'Wait,' said Mina.

Then a deep vice said, 'Salaam Alaikum.'

Jack passed the phone to Mina and nodded.

'Papa?'

The now standing group of friends listened, as Mina spoke to her father. Sarmad, next to her, translated her words swiftly and quietly. After a few minutes she closed down the call and passed the phone back to Ian. 'He will be here as soon as he can. He was upset and worried about me, since I was taken from the hospital a few days ago. He asked many questions, but I told him to come quickly. He will be here soon.'

'Thanks, doc,' said Jack smiling, then turning to Tom, said quietly, 'get the guys on stand-by. Let's hope we only have one truck and one man show up. Anything else and we need to be ready.'

Tom nodded and then moved round the group quietly giving instructions to take up defensive positions, should the arrival of the truck and Mina's father be more than was expected.

It was almost noon, the sun was high in the sky and a warm wind blew hard from the south kicking up dust and sand in its wake. Steve was watching the road and had the binoculars up to his eyes, when he said, 'There's a truck turning off the main road now.'

'Just one vehicle?' said Tom.

'One truck only,' answered Steve, passing the field-glasses to Tom.

'Okay,' said Jack, 'everyone in position.'

Mina stood at the edge of the small clump of trees, as the truck bounced across the barren landscape towards the olive grove; the dust cloud behind it blowing away to the north in the warm mid-day air. As the vehicle came closer it slowed down and moved steadily towards the trees, stopping about twenty yards from the grove. The trailing dust blew away the huge Siddiqi logo could be seen along the side of the van. The door opened and a large heavily built man climbed down from the cab. Mina ran towards him and the two embraced, the big man holding her tightly, tears in his eyes.

The couple walked back into the shade of the olive grove and waited a few seconds until Sarmad came from his concealed position. 'Salaam Alaikum, brother,' he said quietly.

'Alaikum Salaam,' replied the big man, extending his hand.

'You are alone?' asked Sarmad, looking towards the parked truck.

'Yes, yes, alone as Mina asked,' then with shock, he stepped back, as the rest of the group revealed themselves.

'Do not be afraid, brother. We are friends,' said Sarmad as the strangers crowded around him.

'These men are the ones who rescued me from the terrorists, papa. They are my friends. This is my father, Majid al Siddiqi.'

Chapter Twenty Four
'The Farm'

Sarmad and Mina were in the cab with her father Majid;
the rest of the team had piled into the back of the truck,
ready for anything.

'This is a brand new truck,' said Tom, 'the doc's
father must be doing okay.'

'Just as well,' said Kevin, 'we don't want to have to
drive to the border in some knackered old piece of junk.'

'I'm not looking forward to driving to the bloody
border in anything,' grumbled Danny.

'Moan, moan, moan,' said Steve, as he slapped his
friend on the back.

Once off the rough terrain and back on the main road,
the ride became smooth and swift as Majid put his foot
down and increased speed along the highway.

'Sarmad?' said Jack quietly into his throat mic.

'Yes, boss?'

'Not too fast. Tell him to take it easy. We don't want
to attract attention.'

'Yes, boss.'

A few seconds later the truck slowed and began
travelling at the same speed as the rest of the midday
traffic. It was hot and there was little fresh air in the back
of the vehicle, but the ride was not uncomfortable and
twenty five minutes later the big truck slowed and came
to a stop. The guys in the back all had their weapons
trained on the rear doors as they were slowly opened;

then lowered the their guns as Sarmad's smiling face appeared, It's okay,' he said, as he waved them out.

The truck had been parked inside a large warehouse and the big double doors had been closed and secured. Tom looked around the large and relatively new warehouse then said, Steve, Dan, Kevin, Santosh, check the perimeter, have a good look round.'

The four split into two teams and moved away from the group in silence, Kevin and Santosh towards the main doors and Steve and Danny to the rear of the cavernous building.

'You will be safe here until you leave,' said Majid, with Sarmad translating.

Jack nodded and smiled, 'Thank you, sir, but we're gonna need your help to get us across the border as well.'

Sarmad continued the translation, 'He will do anything you ask. You have saved his daughter's life; he is ever in your debt. But he also asks a service from you.'

'Go on?' replied Jack,

'He wants us to take his daughter out of the country. He said she will not be safe here now.'

Through the dusty window at the front of the building, Kevin could see two more large warehouses. There were a dozen or more workers moving in and out, as they unloaded a large truck. A forklift was kicking up dust as it spun round with a pallet piled high with cardboard boxes. No one seemed to be interested in the warehouse the team was hiding in. Santosh checked a small access door cut into the main doors and found it secure. At the back of the warehouse were another two trucks, the Siddiqi logo emblazoned along the side of the trailer; their rear doors open and the interiors empty. Steve cautiously walked up a flight of stairs to a mezzanine, on which stood a large office and what appeared to be a small store room, both of which were locked. Below the mezzanine Danny was checking two more offices and what looked like a new toilet and shower facility. He checked a sturdy rear door and found it to be securely locked and bolted from the inside.

Returning to the main group the four men nodded confirmation the warehouse was secure.

Ian had been checking their position on the GPS, as Sarmad continued to translate Majid's words.

'I will bring food for you all shortly and then we can discuss how we will get you across the border.'

'Thank you, sir,' said Tom.

'Yes, thank you,' added Jack with a hand shake.

'My workers know that my daughter was taken from the hospital. She cannot be seen here or there may be talk,' then turning to Mina he said, 'I will bring fresh clothes that are suitable for you to travel in. You must go with these men when they leave.'

The doctor nodded to her father, then turned to Jack and Tom, 'is this possible? I can leave Syria with you?'

Before they could answer Sarmad spoke, 'You can leave with us and come to Iraq. I will make sure you are safe in Erbil. I can even arrange for a position at the General Hospital if you wish?'

Mina looked at her father and then turning back to Sarmad said, 'Shukran, sidi, you are very kind. You are all very kind.'

'We've gotta get out of here and across the border first though,' said Jack.

An hour later Majid returned to the warehouse driving a small covered Toyota pickup truck. Once inside with the main doors closed and secured; he went to the back of the vehicle and began unloading several containers of food. Sarmad and Santosh had set up a small counter, using some packing cases and pallets. Majid quickly unloaded the containers while Sarmad helped him place the food on the makeshift table.

'This is the food we provide for my workers,' translated Sarmad, 'it is basic, but fresh cooked and wholesome. There is lamb tagine and grilled chicken, buttered couscous and fresh bread. Here is fresh fruit and more water and juices. There is plenty for you I hope? Please, you are welcome, you are my guests. Please eat.'

The smell from the cooked food filled the warehouse and after several days of energy bars and dried rations the group moved swiftly onto the welcome feast before them.

'Grubs up,' said Danny, as he homed in on the pile of steaming chicken.

Sarmad quickly filled a plate and passed it to Mina, as the rest of the group tucked into the delicious fare.

After they'd all eaten, the food containers were loaded back into the pickup. Majid Siddiqi stood in the centre of the group and, with Sarmad translating, began, 'So, my friends we must think about tomorrow. It will take two hours to get to the border and perhaps another half hour to get to the place you wish to be in Turkey. We should leave another half hour for any problems on the road, so three hours in total. We will leave here at six o-clock in the morning if that is acceptable?'

'That's fine Majid,' said Jack. 'The sooner we are out of Syria the better for us. But is there no way we can leave today?'

'We can leave today, but the terrorists may still be looking for you. I think you will be safer to hide today and leave at first light tomorrow. But you are in charge, sidi, if you wish to go today. we go.'

Jack turned to Tom and the rest of the guys. 'He has a point. The group that headed south after us will now realise they were on a wild goose chase and will most likely be back at their compound and planning searches in the area. I say we lay low until morning. Any thoughts?'

'I agree,' said Tom, 'smart to hold up and wait.'

'You're the, boss,' said Santosh, 'I go with you.'

'Nae problem fer me, Jack,' said Ian.

Steve and Danny nodded, as did Kevin and Sarmad.

'Okay then, tomorrow morning it is,' confirmed Jack. He then turned to Sarmad, 'Ask Majid how he plans to get us across the border please?'

'We will use two of these new trucks. We will load them with cargo; I have dried fruit and dates ready to go to Turkey. We will conceal you behind the cargo. It is very rare we are searched at the border now, as I have good relations with the Turkish border control. They are easy to bribe and I have not had any problems for many months now.'

'Who will drive?' asked Jack.

'I will drive one and my son will drive the other,' answered Majid.

'Okay, sounds good,' said Tom.

'Yeah, that's fine. Keep it in the family,' said Jack with a grin.

'Very well, I will leave you now and arrange for the cargo to be loaded into the trucks. You will need to conceal yourselves while the goods are brought into the warehouse,' then handing a set of keys to Sarmad, Majid continued, 'you can hide in the office above, no one will come there.'

'Shukran,' said Sarmad.

'Thank you for all you have done for us, sir,' said Jack.

After Sarmad had translated, Majid looked at the group of foreigners and smiled, 'It is I who must thank you, my friends. You have saved my daughter. It will break my heart to see her leave. But I will be happy she is safe and out of Syria.'

'She will be across the border in Iraq my friend,' said Sarmad, 'it is not impossible for you to come to Erbil to see her, so do not worry. It is not goodbye, inshallah.'

Mina crossed to her father and they both embraced. The big man held his daughter tightly as she turned her face upwards to kiss his cheek.

'Okay, my friends, I will return shortly, so now please conceal yourselves.'

The pickup backed out and the doors were closed and secured. Jack turned to Mina and said, 'Don't you want to see your mother, doc?'

'My mother is dead, Jack. She died when I was born. I was brought up by my father and brother.'

'I'm sorry,' said Jack, 'it must have been very difficult?'

'No, not really. My father is a wonderful man. It was he who helped and supported me when I said I wanted to be a doctor, when I told him I wanted to become a doctor to help stop women dying in childbirth.'

Jack nodded and smiled. 'I'm sure you're gonna have a great career, doc.'

'Okay,' shouted Tom, 'let's get all the gear upstairs and out of sight.'

It was getting dark by the time Majid's workers had finished moving the pallets of cargo into the warehouse. Jack and the team had watched from the confines of the mezzanine office in silence, as Majid directed his workforce swiftly and efficiently. Just before six pm a twenty seater crew bus pulled up in the yard. A few moments later and after shaking hands with their boss, the band of workers all piled onto the bus. Once the bus was out of sight, the big Syrian signalled to the office and a few seconds later Jack, Tom and the rest of the group came down the stairs and across to meet Majid and the man at his side.

'Salaam Alaikum,' said the man, as he extended his hand to Sarmad.

'Alaikum Salaam,' replied Sarmad, as he shook the man's hand.

'This is my brother, Karim,' said Mina, embracing him.

'Thank you for saving my sister,' said Karim in perfect English, 'you are welcome to our home. My father has told me of your plans to leave Syria. We will do everything we can to help you escape safely. We cannot thank you enough for what you have done.'

Chapter Twenty Five
'Warehouse & Farmhouse'

It took almost an hour to load the cargo into the two big container trucks. Majid supervised the loading, leaving a small access route between the pallets.

'We will close-up this area in the morning once we have you all concealed,' translated Sarmad.

'Okay, thank you Majid,' said Jack, 'we'll see you in the morning, sir.'

'Inshallah, Inshallah,' said the big Syrian. Then, turning to his daughter, he embraced her and whispered something into her ear. She stretched up and kissed one cheek as she stroked the other. Karim hugged his sister and said. 'Good night. Try and sleep, tomorrow is an important day in your life sister. God bless.'

After the two men had left and the small access door had been secured, Jack said, 'Steve, Danny, Kev, Santosh, take a look around outside. Let's get a full feel for the surrounding terrain in case we need to abandon this place in a hurry.'

The four men collected their weapons and moved to the rear of the warehouse, after looking through the small window they quietly opened the back door and slipped out into the darkness.

'Doc, you should sleep in one of the driver's cabs tonight. Sarmad, stay close to her,' said Jack. 'Tom, when the guys get back, post guards, two men per hour as usual. You and I'll take the first watch.'

* * *

Before he had spoken with the young goatherd Walid
Mansoori had sent Jack's guard, Farad south to search
for the infidels who had taken his boss Hassan al
Hamady.

'The destruction of the main bridge over the
Euphrates may be a decoy, but we cannot be sure,'
Mansoori had told Farad. 'You will take twenty men and
cross the river via at the old bridge, then proceed south
as fast as you can for one hundred kilometres. If you
find nothing you will return to the compound.'

Farad had been relieved to be given the task of
recovering Hamady and recapturing Jack Castle. 'If they
have gone south, we will find them, sidi, have no fear,'
he said to Mansoori confidently.

That was earlier in the day and now Farad and his
twenty men, after an unsuccessful two hundred kilometre
round trip and a problematic crossing of a traffic-choked
bridge, had returned to the compound. Only four
terrorists remained in the farmhouse when Farad and his
men arrived.

'Where is Captain Mansoori?' he said.

'We do not know, sidi,' answered one of the men,
'we have heard nothing from him all day.'

'But there has been talk of a battle, east of the city,
below the escarpment,' said another.

'And you cowards are here, not with your brothers at
the escarpment?'

'We were told to wait for your return,' said a third
fearfully.

Farad turned to one of his men, 'Hamid, take a vehicle and these four cowards to the escarpment; report back to me here. Go now, go quickly.'

* * *

Steve, Danny, Kevin and Santosh came back from their reconnaissance. After drinking some water Steve said, 'It's a big place, these three warehouses and some kind of fruit processing production plant. There's a big farmhouse on the other side of the production plant with several smaller outbuildings and a large generator house.'

'There's a large lake further on past the farmhouse,' added Kevin. 'It looks to be the main source for the irrigation to the orchards and fields. Majid's got a big place here.'

'He also has a couple of pickups and a nice Landcrusier in the yard as well,' said Santosh.

'Looks to be a pretty big operation,' said Steve, 'apart from that, no security issues. If we had to make a run for it we could use the pickups and Landcrusier.'

'Okay, guys,' said Jack, 'good recon, well done. Tom and I are gonna take first watch; we'll wake Danny and Steve in a couple of hours. Everyone try and get some rest.'

* * *

'Captain Mansoori and his men are all dead,' said Hamid, 'there are also the remains of a helicopter which our brothers must have shot down.'

'Allah o Akbah,' shouted several of the men standing round Farad.

'Silence. Hamid, after prayers you will return to the escarpment with these four cowards and bury all our brothers, you will take two more men with you.'

'Inshallah, sidi,' said Hamid, 'but there was something else, sidi.'

'What?'

'Our brothers' weapons were missing, all their weapons and ammunition had gone. Is that not strange, sidi?'

'You said there was a helicopter; could you see if there were any bodies in the wreckage?

'Five bodies, sidi, two in the cockpit and three in the cabin.'

'The usual air crew for a Blackhawk is two pilots and two gunners' said Farad, a look of concern on his face.

'What are you thinking, sidi?'

'I am not sure yet, but yes, something is strange, Hamid.'

Turning to look out of the window Farad watched the wisps of cloud move slowly across the face of the moon. He was silent for several seconds and then said, 'We must find the doctor. I do not know which hospital she was taken from, but we must find her. You will split into five groups and go to each of the five city hospitals. Find her address and then contact me here.'

Once prayers were over Hamid took his team to the escarpment and the other groups left the compound to find the home of Doctor Mina Siddiqi.

Farad and two remaining men stayed at the farmhouse to wait for news. One man went to make tea, while the other sat with Farad.

'You have assumed command of our group very well, Farad. You have the strength to be a good leader,' he said.

'Inshallah,' said Farad, 'Inshallah.'

'What made you join the ISIL brotherhood, sidi?' asked the man.

Farad looked at his companion then turned to the window again. The clouds had gone from the moon and the night sky was clear. 'I was born in Baghdad and when the American coalition came to Iraq, we thought life would be better for us after Saddam was removed. But the coalition only made the country worse. My older brother was approached after prayers one day. A man who had come from Afghanistan was in Baghdad and was talking with many of the younger men in the mosques. He spoke of the freedom which the true faith brings and how we should take up arms to rid the country, and Islam, of the foreign pestilence. I was not convinced and I left Baghdad to go to university in Damascus, but my brother wanted to fight the infidels. He joined a group of men in Sadr City in Baghdad. Sadr City in 2008 was a rebel stronghold and the security forces very rarely entered that part of the city. My brother became a team leader and one day he was given a mission to arrange and execute a plan to kidnap some foreign security personnel. He had put a dozen men together and had blocked the motorway to the airport. Two British security vehicles had been forced off the main motorway and into the narrow streets of Sadr. After much shooting my brother and his men finally trapped the two vehicles.'

Farad turned from the window and looked at the young man, a smile on his face. 'My brother was always a Manchester United supporter and always wore the red shirt of United. I can remember him shouting at the television when he watched them play soccer, *Come on you reds,* he would shout, *Come on you reds.'*

'Yes. So you said he had the British trapped. What happened next?'

'Yes, they were trapped and his mission was to capture and kidnap them, so he did not want them dead of course. He went out into the street in front of the two vehicles. The men inside had come out and were hiding behind the big armoured doors of the Landcruisers. My brother had a white flag of truce and he wore his red Manchester United shirt. He called to them to surrender, but they did not listen. He called again, but this time the infidels shot him in the chest and killed him while holding the white flag. When I was told of his death it was then my heart turned to revenge and I left university and found the ISIL brotherhood.'

Chapter Twenty Six
'Where is Mina Siddiqi'

Jack did not get any sleep, even though he'd made a reasonably comfortable make-shift bed of pallets and cardboard cartons. A little after five-o-clock he stood up and stretched his back, a sharp pain in his still injured ribs causing him to wince slightly. Tom was already up and about and was coming from the toilet and shower room at the back of the warehouse. He waved to Jack as he approached and said, 'Get any sleep?'

'No, nothing, How about you?'

'A couple of hours, no more.'

The rest of the team was stirring and then Sarmad appeared from the cab of the big truck, followed by Doctor Mina Sidiqi. Everyone congregated around the makeshift table and helped themselves to fresh fruit, bread and cheese, water and fruit juices, that Majid had provided the night before. The chatter in the group was light-hearted and the mood confident. Everyone turned to the small access door as Majid and his son Karim entered. They carried two large metal canisters and a tube of paper cups, the smell of fresh coffee identified the contents of the canisters.

'Coffee,' said Danny with delight.

After the welcome hot fresh coffee had been consumed, Jack said, 'Time to go, gentlemen. Sarmad, please tell Majid that you will ride up front in the first truck with him. Santosh speaks Arabic so he will ride in the second cab with Karim. We need to have a couple of our guys on the outside and armed, just in case.'

The translation made and understood, Majid said, 'Now, please get into the back of the trucks. Karim and I will then close up the passage way and conceal you.'

It was five-to-six when the two sixteen wheeler trucks rolled out of the Sidiqi warehouse, the big tyres kicking up a small dust cloud as they accelerated away from the yard.

There was plenty of room in the back of the trailers so the ride was reasonably comfortable. Jack, Ian, Kevin and Mina, were concealed in the first vehicle and Tom, Steve and Danny in the second.

'Tom, Santosh, Sarmad, radio check,' said Jack into his throat mic.

Tom's voice came back first, followed by Sarmad and Santosh from their respective cabs.

The sun had breached the horizon and an early morning mist was clearing when Majid rolled off the dusty access road from his farm and onto the main highway to the north and the Turkish border.

* * *

Hamid and his team of grave diggers had been back at the ISIL farmhouse for the last couple of hours. Three of the five groups which Farad had dispatched to the city hospitals had also returned with no information about the home or whereabouts of Doctor Mina Sidiqi, much to the anger of Farad. The assembled terrorists were in the middle of morning prayers when, at a few minutes past six, the fourth team's vehicle sped through the open gates of the compound and skidded to a halt in a swirling cloud of dust and sand. The team leader rushed into the farmhouse eager to pass on his information to Farad, but seeing his comrades at prayer, waited impatiently for them to finish their devotions.

Farad stood up, folded his prayer mat and then pulled on his boots, as the team leader came into the makeshift mosque. Turning to the young Syrian, Farad said, 'Salam Alaikum, you have news of the Sidiqi bitch?'

'Alaikum Salam, brother. Yes, yes, we have discovered her address, sidi. It was not easy, as no one at the hospital wanted to give us any information, but they were persuaded once we shot one of them in the foot.' said the team leader, a smug grin on his sweaty face.

'I'm not interested in how you obtained the information you fool. Where does this woman live?' snapped Farad.

'Yes, sidi, excuse me.'

'Well then?' snarled Farad.

'Her father has a large farm and processing plant north of Al Raqqah. Apparently it is well known in the city. He is a very successful farmer and exporter, the doctor lives there.'

'Exporter?' said Farad.

'Yes, sidi.'

'And you know the exact location of this farm?'

'Yes, sidi. It is off the main north highway to the Turkish border, Inshallah.'

'Quickly, assemble all the men, everyone, all fully armed, we must leave at once.'

It took almost twenty minutes for Farad and his four vehicles to travel the busy ring road to the north of the city. The early morning traffic was busy as usual, but the fast moving convoy, lights flashing and horns blaring, forced its way through the civilian vehicles, trucks and carts with no regard for the safety of the other road users. By six twenty five they had entered the gates to the big farm, pulling up to the farmhouse in a flurry of sand and dust. The doors were locked, but Farad's men wasted no time in kicking open the big wooden portal. Farad waited anxiously until the half dozen men returned from the interior of the building.

'There's no one here, sidi,' shouted the first man out.

Turning to look at the rest of the property, Farad saw several men unloading a large van with the *SIDDIQI & SON logo* along the side. As he climbed back into his Landcruiser he pointed to the group of watchers and shouted, 'There.'

Majid's workers looked fearful as the band of heavily armed men surrounded them.

'Who is in charge here?' said Farad in a quiet voice.

No one spoke and then Farad drew his side-arm, cocked the weapon and pointed it at the head of the nearest worker.

'I have no time to waste on asking questions twice. Who is in charge here?'

An older man stepped forward and said, 'I am the foreman, sidi. Mohamed al Jebel.'

'Salam Alaikum, Mohamed,' said Farad, If I get answers to my questions quickly you have my word no one will be hurt. Where is Doctor Mina Siddiqi?'

'We have not seen her for several days, sidi,' replied the foreman.

'Where is her father?'

'He is not here, sidi.'

Farad lowered his weapon and shot the worker nearest to him in the thigh. The young man screamed in agony as he rolled on the floor holding his leg, blood streaming from the gunshot wound. A couple of his fellow workers moved to help the whimpering man, but stopped as Farad's men turned their weapons on them.

'One last time,' said Farad, his voice menacing, the gun again pointed at the young man's head.

'The boss left this morning with two trucks. We loaded cargo for Turkey last night. He was leaving as we arrived this morning.'

'How do you know he was going to Turkey?'

'I completed the documentation, sidi. It was an unexpected trip. The cargo is bound for a town called Garac, a few miles north of the border in Turkey.'

'What time did he leave, Mohamed?'

'Six-o-clock, sidi.'

Farad looked at the Rolex on his wrist and smiled as he thought of Jack Castle, the infidel he had taken it from. 'Twenty five to seven,' he said, 'they have thirty five minutes start on us. We need to stop those trucks.'

'But, Farad, how do we know who is in them?' said Hamid.

'You said our brothers who were killed at the escarpment had no weapons.'

'Peace be upon their souls,' said Hamid, 'yes, yes, no weapons. What does that mean, sidi?'

'Blackhawks always travel in pairs. The Americans never send only one helicopter, always two.'

'So the infidels were rescued by the second helicopter and are probably back in Iraq by now,' said Hamid.'

'Maybe,' said Farad, as he walked quickly back to the vehicles, 'but why bother to take our brothers weapons?'

'I don't know, sidi, why?'

'Because they needed them. They needed extra weapons. Because they never left in the second helicopter. They are still in Syria and are being helped to escape by Mina Sidiqi's father. We have to stop those trucks. Let's move.'

Chapter Twenty Seven
'Highway North'

The British military base on Cyprus, was established in the 1950's as support for British troops during the Suez Crisis. Now known as RAF Akrotiri, it is a strategic military location in the Mediterranean for the British Air Force, and home to three squadrons of Tornado aircraft, several Sea King helicopters, a reasonable contingent of Royal Marines plus a small detachment of the 22nd Parachute regiment, Special Air Service.

In the flight briefing room Captain Mike Chalmers and his co-pilot David Winston listened as the duty operations officer outlined their morning's mission into Turkey. Behind the pilots sat six very fit looking men in desert camouflage uniform; behind the soldiers stood Mathew Sterling. As the briefing finished and everyone was leaving the room Mathew nodded to the young SAS officer and said, 'A word please, Lieutenant.'

'Certainly, sir,' said the officer, 'just a second please,' then turning to his departing men said, 'I'll catch up with you in a few minutes, Sergeant.'

'Okay, boss.'

'What can I do for you, sir?'

'It's Gareth isn't it?'

'Yes, sir, Gareth Mallory.'

'I just wanted a quick word, Gareth,' said Mathew quietly,' the men you are going in to extract are private civilian security as you know.'

'Yes, sir.'

'As you also know, it is rather unusual for the British military to intervene and undertake such a mission as this, but these men have vital intelligence about ISIL that we must recover.   One of them is actually a veteran from your regiment, Gareth. Captain Jack Castle.'

'Yes, I've heard of him, sir. He was one of the team that rescued the hostages from the Iranian Embassy siege, back in the eighties.'

'Indeed he was and many other skirmishes since,' said Matt with a smile, 'anyway, Gareth, I just wanted you to understand why we are going in for these guys'

'No need to explain, sir. We do what we're told. But don't worry; we'll get them and your intelligence out. Now if you will excuse me, sir, I must join my men. We have wheels up in twenty minutes.'

'Yes of course, thank you, Lieutenant,' as they shook hands Mathew said, 'good luck and be safe.'

* * *

Majid's new trucks were not refrigerated, but they did have air-conditioning to ensure his food product cargos were held at the appropriate temperature while in transit; so it was not too uncomfortable for Jack, Tom and the rest of the guys to be holed up in the trailers. The journey to the border was an easy one, made on a reasonably well maintained road that ran the length of Syria from north to south and although the highway was busy, the small convoy managed to maintain a steady seventy kilometres an hour on its journey north.

'Sarmad, come back,' said Jack into his throat mic.
'Yes, boss?'

'How's it looking out there?'

'Okay, boss. The road is very busy, but we are making good time according to Majid.'

'Great, cheers, buddy. Tom, come back.'

'Copy, Jack.'

'How you guys doing back there?'

'We're fine, mate. Danny is sleeping and snoring his head off, but apart from that, okay,' said Tom. He looked at his watch, 'We've been travelling for over an hour, so we should be at least halfway to the border,' he said.

'Yeah, looks like we're on schedule,' said Jack.

Ian tore open the plastic around a case of water and passed a bottle each to Mina, Jack and Kevin. Gulping it down, Kevin said, 'A little on the warm side, but still does the job.'

'It'll nae be long till its cold beer, Kev,' said Ian.

'How you feeling doc, you okay?' said Jack.

'I'm fine, Jack, don't worry.'

'So, boss,' said Kevin, 'you haven't told us how those bastards, oh sorry doc, scuse me.'

'No problem, Kevin,' said Mina smiling, 'they are bastards.'

'Right, yeah,' said Kevin, a little surprised at the doctor's use of the word, 'as I was saying, boss; you haven't told us how they picked you up?'

'Not now, buddy, maybe later.'

'I'd be interested to know what happened, Jack,' said Mina, 'Sarmad told me you let yourself be kidnapped. Why would anyone actually do that?'

'It's a long story.'

'We have another hour or so to travel,' said Mina smiling.

'Okay, I'll try and make it as brief as I can. We got intelligence that The Fox, that is the code name, sorry, was the codename, the intelligence services used for Hassan al Hamady, he was second in command of ISIL.'

'Oh my god,' said Mina, 'I never realised he was that important.'

'Exactly, that's why we came to capture him,' said Kevin, 'oh sorry, boss, go on.'

'And tae get Jack back of course,' said Ian.

'Yeah, so as I was saying. The idea was for me to be kidnapped by ISIL, so The Fox would come to the location I was being held. We knew he would try extracting a ransom for me, but we knew that was not the only thing he wanted; he'd want to execute me himself. Anyway the plan was for my guys to mount the rescue mission and capture Hamady at the same time.'

'So you let yourself be taken just to lure out Hamady?' said Mina.

'We got information that The Fox had put out a fatwah on me, my friends and our families.'

'Why?' said Mina.

'Last year we were on a mission in the Iraqi desert and we were attacked by ISIL. In that firefight we killed Hamady's eldest son.'

'So that was the reason he wanted to kill you and your families?'

'Half the reason,' said Jack, 'a few weeks later he sent a hit squad to kidnap my wife, fiancé as she was then. They took her from my father-in-law's island and were heading back up the Gulf on a dhow. We mounted a rescue mission and assaulted the ship.'

'Did you get her back?'

'Yes, we did, and she's fine. But during that rescue Hamady's other son was killed. So that must have driven him crazy. He wanted me and everyone involved in the deaths of his sons killed, as well as our families.'

'I understand now,' said Mina, 'so you allowed yourself to be kidnapped to protect your family and your friends.'

'Pretty much, yeah. Crazy eh?' said Jack.

'But how did your friends know where to find you? You could have been anywhere.'

'We had a little technological help with that; needless to say my guys knew where I was at all times.'

'So The Fox is dead and you are all now safe?'

'For now, I hope,' said Jack smiling.

'Okay, I understand why you wanted to be taken, but how did they find you? You didn't walk up to them and say hello, I'm Jack Castle.'

'It might have been easier,' said Jack grinning and holding his still aching ribs, 'I had to make it appear they'd found me, otherwise they may have smelled a rat and deduced it was a setup and I could have ended up dead there and then.'

'So where did they find you?'

'Sarmad and I went to Aleppo. Our cover story was to set up a security service in the city for expatriate oil field personnel. We booked into the Aleppo Sheraton where most of the expats hang out and essentially made ourselves highly conspicuous.'

'And how did you do that?'

'We were loud, we pretended to be drunk a lot and we caused quite a bit of upset in the dining room and bars. It was fun actually.'

'But Sarmad doesn't drink alcohol, does he?'

'No, and nor do I. Pretended to be drunk I said.'

'Ahh, okay,' she said smiling.

'Anyway, we'd been there four days and on the evening of the fourth day we went out to the car park, loud and obnoxious as usual. We'd hired an old Mercedes and as we walked, staggered, towards it; we saw an old van parked alongside our Merc, with a couple of guys arguing at the back door of the van. The plan was that Sarmad would not be taken whatever happened. They would have killed him outright and as this looked like it could be the snatch, I sent him back to the hotel.'

'Oh my god, this is like something from the television.'

'Errm, perhaps, I still have to tell Nicole all this. Not looking forward to that.'

'Who's Nicole?'

'My wife. Anyway, I stagger towards the Merc and start fumbling for the keys when this guy comes round from the front of the van and in broken English tells me I shouldn't be driving. As I turn to him he hits me right in the face; that's it of course and I start to put up a bit of a drunkards' resistance. The two guys from the back of the van join in giving me a good kicking and then they all drag me to the back of the van. I'm playing my part of the drunken infidel trying to fight off these three jokers, but they bundle me into the back and slam the door, unfortunately that's when I injured my hand. The two guys in the back tie me up and put a bag over my head. Quite a while later and after a very uncomfortable journey, I'm dragged out of the van and thrown into the room you saw me in. Job done, I'm captured.'

* * *

The convoy of four ISIL vehicles was moving very fast along the northbound side of the highway. Farad, in the lead Landcruiser constantly yelling at his driver and forcing him to take unnecessary risks on the busy road; the three other vehicles trying hard to maintain the fast pace set by the Landcruiser. They were travelling at over a hundred and twenty kliks, and weaving dangerously in and out of the slower moving trucks and vehicles when the last truck in their convoy clipped a small Lada saloon. The tiny car spun out of control and ran off the side of the road coming to a stop in an all-consuming cloud of sand; but the young inexperienced truck driver lost control of the heavy vehicle. His truck swerved and rammed into the side of a large sixteen wheeler, then bounced off and across the central reservation, smashing the steering and front suspension as it bounced over the high curb and on into the path of the oncoming traffic. The young driver, now in a state of total panic could do nothing without the steering and the out of control vehicle hit another small car, then ran over a couple on a motorbike; the truck bouncing as the bike and bodies went under its wheels.

Cars and buses swerved, their brakes screeching as they fought to avoid ramming into the ISIL vehicle. It was not so for the huge mobile crane that ploughed into the stricken truck, its massive protruding steel jib, with the big hanging block and hook went right through the passenger cabin like a knife through butter, decapitating two of the terrorists and throwing the other two out and under the wheels of the skidding vehicles.

'Farad,' yelled one of the men in the third vehicle.

Picking up the radio handset Farad said, 'What is it?'

'Farad, sidi, we have lost the last truck, it has crashed. We must see if our brothers are hurt.'

'If they are hurt or dead it is the will of Allah, we will not stop.'

'But, sidi….'

The radio went dead.

Chapter Twenty Eight
'The Border'

The border crossing area on the Syria side is a shambolic location. The Syrian check point and control is no more than a series of porta-cabins, a few old and unused buildings, some disgusting public toilets and a large fenced off compound for vehicles which have been impounded for one reason or another. The approach road to the crossing is flanked by large and small roadside shops and stalls, selling everything from livestock to spare parts. Many of the stalls are makeshift catering outlets providing all kinds of kebabs, barbecues and sweet-meats. The risk to health in eating anything from these vendors being equal to that of Russian roulette

There are two lanes going out of the country and two lanes coming in; the first and most efficient is for commercial vehicles exporting or importing cargo, the other for private citizens' cars and vehicles. The commercial   lane is efficient because the drivers and owners of the cargo know they need to make a payment at the border to ensure their trucks are not held up and subsequently processed swiftly. Private cars on the other hand, must wait for several hours before they can be allowed out or in to the country.

Off to the side of the main vehicle control is a fenced-off pedestrian facility for those making the journey on foot. The queue of people waiting to be processed and allowed through the border and into Turkey stretched back for more than a mile. Men, women and children, their meagre belonging wrapped in sheets and worn out old carpets waited in the heat of the morning sun. Babies in pushchairs, old prams and homemade carts cried and whimpered as the temperature rose. Tempers amongst the impatient throng wore out and gave way to minor arguments and brawls. An argument at a roadside vendor's stall resulted in the barbecue being knocked over causing a fire that quickly grew to engulf the small tented structure. The futile attempts by the stall holder to extinguish and save the source of his livelihood delighted the bored congregation and cheers and jibes went up at the hapless vendor's misfortune. But for Majid's trucks the transition was expedited with relevant ease and they were through the border process and into Turkey in less than thirty minutes.

* * *

The ISIL convoy slowed down as it approached the rear of the queue waiting to cross the border. In the lead vehicle Farad picked up the radio and clicked the button, 'Hamid.'

'Yes, sidi?'

'Drive onto the desert, move along the queue. See if the Sidiqi trucks are still here. Go quickly.'

'Inshallah, sidi.'

Farad watched as his second vehicle moved off the road and drove out into the desert about fifty metres, then ran parallel with the line of waiting commercial vehicles. In less than five minutes Hamid was back and pulled up alongside Farad's Landcruiser and got out. 'No trucks with *SIDDIQI & SON* on them, sidi.'

'They cannot be too far in front of us now,' said Farad, his face stern and determined.

'We cannot cross into Turkey, sidi. Not with weapons,' said Hamid.

Farad turned, his eyes wild, his voice shaking, 'The infidels are in those trucks. I will not stop at the border and lose them. They will pay for taking Hassan al Hamady. They will pay for the killing of Walid Mansoori. They will pay for the killing of all our brothers. Get back in your vehicles and follow me.'

* * *

The Sea King was now in Turkish air space and no external radio transmissions were to be made until they arrived at the rendezvous, even then communications were to be in code.

The internal communication on the aircraft however was not subject to this protocol. Over the clatter of the big rotors Lieutenant Gareth Mallory had to almost shout into his throat mic, 'ETA at the landing zone, sir?' he said to the pilot.

'We should be on location as planned, Lieutenant. I hope they're waiting for us. We are pretty much at the limit of this aircraft's range, so we will not have a lot of time to wait around.'

'Roger that, sir. Thank you.'

Mallory looked at his watch and then turned to the sergeant next to him, leaning in close and shouting above the engine's noise, he said, 'Thirty minutes, Andy. Weapons check.'

The big sergeant nodded, raised his automatic rifle and tapped the breach twice. The rest of his men began checking weapons, body armour, ammunition and grenades. Two of the six carried hand held rocket launchers; both soldiers carefully checked the highly explosive projectiles were secure and the safety mechanisms were engaged. Each man gave a thumbs-up to the sergeant on completion of the task and the two rocket-carriers went back to playing cards.

* * *

Farad's small convoy had driven fast across the desert running parallel to the two big fences that secured the border between Syria and Turkey. In between the fences was a twenty metre strip of desert designating no-man's land. They had driven east for about three miles and were well out of site of the border crossing when Farad brought the convoy to a sudden halt. 'Here, look. Allah be praised. Both fences have been breached and neither has been repaired. We cross here.'

Hamid left his vehicle and quickly ran across to Farad's. He opened the door as Farad snapped at him, 'What now?'

'Sidi, are you sure we should do this?'

Farad looked into the eyes of the man in front of him and then drew his sidearm. He cocked the weapon and held it to Hamid's forehead, 'You can come with me, brother or die here, the choice is yours.'

Hamid stepped back and nodded, then turned and walked back to his vehicle, shaking his head slowly.

Chapter Twenty Nine
'The Garac Road'

The Sidiqi convoy passed into Turkey without any problems at the border and it had been travelling for several minutes when Jack said into his throat mic, 'Sarmad, come back.'

'Yes, boss?'

'Are we clear of the border area?'

'Yes, boss well clear, we have turned off the main highway and are on the minor road to Garac.'

'Good. Please ask, Majid to pull over and let us out of here, no need to hide now.'

'Okay.'

A few seconds later the squeal of the airbrakes was heard as the big truck slowed down and came to a stop. The cab doors were slammed and Majid's voice was heard chattering in Arabic. The buzz of the cargo lift motor vibrated through the trailer and then the big rear doors were opened, sending a gust of welcome fresh air and beams of sunlight into the dim interior of the trailer. Majid and his son Karim used the heavy duty pallet trolley to carefully manoeuvre the double stacked pallet back onto the cargo lift platform, then turned to the interior to see his daughter coming from behind the other stacks of cargo. She rubbed her eyes as they became accustomed to the bright morning sunlight. Her father embraced her and kissed her cheeks and her brother helped her down from the cargo lift to the sand. Majid stepped down from the platform as Ian, Kevin and then

Jack all appeared from the rear of the trailer, carrying their bags and weapons, smiles on all their faces, as they too jumped down from the trailer.

'Tell me it was not that easy?' said Jack to Sarmad.

'Looks like it boss.'

'Tell your father thank you please, Mina,' said Jack.

Then to everyone's surprise Majid said in stilted English, 'Thank you. Mr Jack.'

Everyone laughed as the words came out in English, the thick Arabic accent distorting them.

'Hey, are we getting outta here today?' shouted Danny, as he banged on the side of their trailer. Once Tom, Steve and Danny had been released from their confinement, Jack turned to Ian and said, 'Better check the GPS, we still have a few miles to go and not long until the chopper.'

'Already on it, boss. 'We have less than five miles along this road and then we turn east for about a mile.'

'Well done, buddy,' said Tom, 'let's get going then.'

It was a tight squeeze to get everyone plus equipment into the cabs. The weapons and bags were stowed on the shelves above the sleeping berth, then Steve, Santosh and Kevin climbed into the bunk area, with Sarmad in the front passenger seat.

'This is all very cosy,' said Steve, laughing, 'good job Danny's not in here with his wind problem.'

In the lead truck they stowed the equipment and weapons in the storage above the berth. Jack, Danny and Tom settled down in the bunk area and Ian took the passenger seat with the GPS equipment. Mina sat between her father and Ian on the carpet covered engine housing. The air brakes squealed as they were released, the big engines growled as Majid and Karim eased the trucks back onto the road then accelerated towards Garac.

* * *

Farad's three vehicles had rolled over the broken border fences without any problems and were now heading north-west at top speed towards the Garac road. Along with Jack Castle's Rolex, Farad had helped himself to the infidel's smartphone and it was this he now held in his hand. He had the ordinance survey map of Southern Turkey spread out on his lap, but reading it was difficult as the big Landcruiser bounced over the desert. The smartphone had a GPS application into which Farad had typed in Garac. 'Stay on the desert and continue north-west, we should hit the Garac road in a few minutes,' he snapped at the driver.

The dust cloud from the lead vehicle made it difficult for the following vehicles to see so, they moved out of the cloud and took up position's each side of Farad. The driver of the big Landcruiser increased speed as Farad yelled, 'There, look, there. Vehicles on the road. That is the road to Garac.'

In less than a minute the Landcruiser bounced off the desert and onto the road, narrowly missing a battered old mini bus, its feeble horn blaring indignantly.

* * *

Majid slowed down as Mina translated Ian's instruction, 'Turn off to the right, just after this abandoned petrol station,' she told her father.

Ian turned to the guys in the back and said, 'The rendezvous is aboot half a mile off this road. We'll be there in a wee minute.'

'Yes!' said Danny, then leaning forward, he extended his hand palm up, as Ian leant back and slapped it.

'We did it, Tom. Thank you,' said Jack as he shook hands with his friend.

Chapter Thirty
'What Kept You?'

Although there was no need to avoid Turkish radar the Sea King had descended from normal flying altitude to two hundred feet, the better for the pilot to have eyes, on any activity on the ground. The rendezvous co-ordinates had been entered to the aircrafts navigational computer and the display was reading fourteen miles out with approximately seven minutes to location. As the Sea King levelled out at two hundred feet, Sergeant Andy Harris pulled open the helicopter's big side door. The welcome morning air filled the interior of the aircraft, as the six man team all strained to see what was waiting for them on the ground.

* * *

The screech and hiss of the air brakes heralded the arrival at the rendezvous point. The two big Sidiqi wagons came to a stop in a swirl of dust and sand that slowly drifted away on the warm morning breeze. Once the dust had cleared, Majid opened the door and dropped down from the cab, then waited to help his daughter, as she unceremoniously clambered over the driver seat and out of the vehicle. Ian was already out and checking the GPS to make sure they were indeed in the correct location, as Jack and Tom struggled out of the small berth area and then waited for Danny to pass down the weapons and equipment. The guys in the second truck had all dismounted and were busy getting equipment and weapons ready for the pickup.

'D'ye want me tae contact the chopper, Jack?' said Ian.

But before Jack could answer, Santosh shouted, 'What the hell is this?'

Everyone turned and looked towards the road and saw the huge dust cloud being kicked up by the three fast approaching vehicles.

'That's fucking trouble,' said Steve.

'Karim, move your wagon alongside this one, fast, give us cover on two sides,' shouted Jack.

Tom had already picked up the sniper rifle and was climbing up onto the roof of Majid's trailer. 'Sarmad,' said Jack, 'get the doc under the trailer, stay with her.'

As Karim's wagon pulled alongside Majid's, Steve said, 'Defensive positions, boss?'

'Defensive positions until we know what we are dealing with. Let's move.'

* * *

Farad picked up the radio mic and screamed into the handset, 'Allah o Akbah. We have them. We have them.'

Hamid came back over the radio, 'Sidi, slow down, we do not know how many there are, do not rush at them.'

As if in answer to Hamid's plea, Farad seemed to calm down and said, 'Position your vehicle to the right of their trucks, Hamid. I will go to the left, last vehicle move to the middle. We will attack them from three directions.' The small convoy split as Farad had directed.

Tom's voice came over the radio, 'They're going for position, gonna hit us on three sides.'

'Conserve ammunition, guys, the chopper should be here soon,' said Jack into his throat mic. Then turning to Ian he grinned and said, 'Now would be a good time to contact Empire.'

The ISIL vehicles screeched to a halt in three equally large clouds of dust and sand. Farad was the first out of his Landcruiser and had begun firing at the trucks even though he could see no one. The other four men with him dismounted and took positions behind the Landcruiser quickly joining in the attack on the Sidiqi wagons. Hamid and his four men brought their weapons to bear and opened fire, as did the five men from the last vehicle. Tom took aim at the nearest vehicle and shot two men in quick succession, before Farad's men trained their fire on him. The thin aluminium roof was no protection from gunfire as the rounds from the terrorists' weapons tore through the side of the trailer. Tom rolled along the roof before taking his next shots. Danny and Steve were behind the big wheels at the rear of Majid's trailer, returning fire accurately and making each round count. Santosh and Kev were behind the cab laying down fire on Hamid and his men. Between them they had hit two men from Farad's team and one from Hamid's, but did not have the angle to bring their weapons to bear on the middle vehicle. Jack and Sarmad, firing from under the big trailer were holding down the guys in the middle vehicle, but that's all they were doing. Tom had moved position and taken two more shots killing two of Hamid's men. Having no more rounds for the sniper rife, he slipped down from the trailer and onto the roof of the cab, then using an AK47 he opened up on the middle truck hitting another of the terrorists.

'Bulldog, Bulldog, this is Empire. We are on your location in sixty seconds, do you copy?'

Ian passed the radio to Jack, 'Empire, this is Bulldog, good to hear from you, sir.'

'Bulldog we see you, please confirm status. You look to be engaged in a firefight.'

'Affirmative, Empire. We are engaged by unknown numbers and low on ammunition. Can you make the extraction, Empire. Over.'

'Negative Bulldog, we cannot land in a hot LZ.'

In the aircraft's cabin Gareth Mallory listened to the radio chatter between the pilot and the team on the ground, then got out of his seat and went up to the flight deck. 'Captain, you need to put me and my team in, sir.'

'Negative, Lieutenant. We are not able to land.'

'Sir, back away to that old petrol station and put us down there. You can land behind it, out of range of their weapons.'

'I can put you down, but we are not able to stay long on the ground. We're almost at our maximum range here, Lieutenant. I can give you ten minutes.'

'Sir, land and shut down your engines, we'll get those guys out. But do not take off without us, sir. If you do, you'd better hope we don't make it out.'

'Are you threatening me, Lieutenant?'

'Absolutely, sir. Now put us in.'

The Sea King banked to the west and gained altitude as it passed over the Garac road, then turning back east it dropped to fifty feet and approached the abandoned petrol station. The dust rose and engulfed the helicopter for a few second until the powerful rotors cleared the landing area. The aircraft was still a few feet in the air when Gareth Mallory dropped from the open door to the ground, quickly followed by Sergeant Andy Harris. The minute the wheels had touched the sand the other four SAS troopers were out and joined Mallory and Harris at the side of the building.

'Two teams, gentlemen,' said Mallory as he assessed the situation through a small pair of binoculars. 'Sergeant, take the left flank. I'll take the middle vehicle. We'll deal with the third in due course. Let's go.'

As the six men set of at a fast sprint, Captain Mike Chalmers shut down the aircrafts' engines and then spoke into the radio, 'Bulldog, Bulldog, this is Empire.'

Over the noise of the gunfire Jack shouted, 'We read you, Empire. Over.'

'Bulldog, you have friendlies approaching from the west. I repeat six friendlies approaching from the west. Over'

'Roger that, Empire.'

Jack stood up and waved to Tom on the roof of the cab, then shouted 'Support coming in from the road.'

Tom gave a thumbs-up and grinned at his old friend, then continued to fire on the middle truck.

Steve and Danny had no ammunition left for their AK's or the machine guns and were now standing and using their side arms. Jack tapped Steve on the shoulder and then pointed to the two small groups of men running across the desert towards their attackers.

Farad was firing indiscriminately at the Siddiqi trucks, screaming obscenities as he reloaded and continued to pour round after round at Jack Castle and the men with him. Two of his team had been killed, he didn't know how many more were dead in the other vehicles, he'd no idea how many infidels were with Castle, yet he continued to curse and fire on the besieged wagons. It was Hamid who saw the men running towards the vehicles, he crawled into his truck, grabbed the radio and yelled into the handset, but it was too late.

Sergeant Harris and his two troopers were a hundred yards from Farad's vehicle when he gave the signal for his men to stop. Instinctively they all dropped to one knee. Harris tapped the young trooper on the shoulder, who quickly unslung the rocket launcher, flipped off the safety mechanism and took aim at the Landcruiser.

The screech of the small rocket as it left the launcher caused Farad to turn, with enough time to see the device hit the back of his vehicle. The projectile exploded, detonating the petrol tank as well. The Landcruiser and the three men around it were immediately engulfed in a huge fireball.

The explosion shocked the men in the middle vehicle and they turned to see their leader's Landcruiser burst into flames. Gareth Mallory and his men were forty yards away when they opened up with their automatic rifles, each sending twelve hundred rounds a minute at the hapless attackers, killing all of them.

In the remaining truck Hamid lay across the driver's seat, his two men still firing on the Sidiqi wagons, 'Get in, get in,' he yelled, as the six SAS men rushed towards them, their weapons on full automatic. He struggled to start the engine, when his men were thrown back by the force of the rounds tearing into their bodies. Bullets thudded into the truck as the engine growled into life. He could not see where he was going, but he pressed his foot hard down on the accelerator as the vehicle quickly reversed away from the oncoming soldiers. Mallory raised his hand as Hamid's truck bounced away over the desert, 'That'll do lads.'

Tom had jumped down from the top of the cab, as Jack and Sarmad scrambled from underneath the trailer. The rest of the team walked out to meet Mallory and his men.

'What kept you?' said Danny, a huge grin on his face, his hand extended to Mallory.

'Sorry old chap, got here as soon as we could. Who's in charge?'

Danny turned as Jack arrived and said, 'This is the, boss.'

'Jack Castle, Lieutenant, excellent timing, sir, thank you.'

As he shook hands with Jack he said, 'Gareth Mallory, we have a ride for you, gentlemen if you're ready to go? But there appears to be more of you than we expected, sir.'

Jack turned to Majid and his son Karim, 'These two gentlemen risked everything to get us out of Syria, but they won't be travelling. The lady however will be.'

Tom shook Majid's hand, 'Thank you for all you've done for us.'

Jack slapped Karim on the back saying, 'Well done, and thank you for everything.'

Thanks and handshakes followed from Steve and the rest of the team as Mallory said, 'We really must go, gentlemen. There's a very twitchy pilot waiting to take us home.'

The left side of Farad's body was black and charred and his clothes had melted into what was left of his flesh. The left side of his face was unrecognisable as human. He lay on the warm sand several yards away from the still smouldering Landcruiser, his lungs burning with each gasp of breath he took. He opened the one eye he had left and through blurred vision saw the group of infidels standing next to the Siddiqi wagons. He felt for his sidearm and with more pain than he had ever felt before managed to draw it from its holster. His breathing was shallow and his vision impaired, as he raised the weapon and pointed it towards the group.

The sound of the gun shot caused everyone to flinch. Sergeant Harris pushed Kevin out the way and fired a short burst into the already dead body of Farad. For a few seconds everyone scanned the carnage around them and then Mallory said, 'That is definitely our cue to get the hell out of here.' Mina quickly hugged her father and kissed his cheek as tears rolled down hers, then hugging her brother said, 'Take care of him.'

The group were already jogging towards the old petrol station as Sarmad took hold of Mina's arm, 'We must go.'

Majid and Karim watched as the band of strangers ran across the desert, taking with them their beloved Mina.

'She will be safe now,' said Karim, as he turned to his father.

Majid nodded, smiled, then dropped to his knees.

'Father!'

Majid's head rolled back as he slumped to the sand.

'Father what is it?' said Karim, as he fell to his knees. He cradled the old man's head in his lap and pulled him close. As he took his hand away he saw the blood. Lifting the crimson soaked shirt he saw the wound in Majid's side.

'I'll get them back. They can help you. Mina will help you.'

Majid held onto his son's arm, 'No she must go. She must live her life safely.'

The sound of the Sea King's engines made them both look towards the old petrol station. Majid looked at his weeping son and then smiled as he saw the helicopter rise into the clear morning sky. They watched together as the aircraft disappeared over the western horizon. As the helicopter vanished the old man's eyes closed.

Chapter Thirty One
'Touch Down'

The Sea King helicopter came slowly in to land, its rotors kicking up dust as the big aircraft descended to the helipad. Mathew Sterling watched from the edge of the flight line as the rotors stopped and the side door was opened. The SAS team disembarked first, quickly followed by Tom and Jack, who stopped to help a woman from the high doorway. The rest of the team piled out carrying various weapons and bags and looking decidedly the worse for wear since the last time he saw them in Erbil.

A dark green British Army Landrover pulled up alongside Mathew and the SAS men piled into the back. Gareth Mallory stopped and shook hands with Mathew, 'Thank you, Lieutenant,' said Matt, 'well done, sir.'

'You're welcome,' said Mallory with a smile and then climbed into the back of the vehicle with his men.

A large canvas covered military truck was parked off to the side of the flight line and Mathew indicated for Jack and the team to board it.

'Great to see you, Jack,' said Mathew, 'really great to see you. Thank God you're all back safe.'

Tom shook Matt's hand, and said, 'Good to be back.'

Mathew shook hands with the rest of the guys, then smiling at Mina said, 'And who's this?'

'This is Doctor Mina Sidiqi,' said Jack, 'she and her father and brother got us across the border. We couldn't leave her in Syria. We're gonna take her to Iraq. She's going to Erbil.'

'A pleasure to meet you, Doctor Sidiqi,' said Mathew still smiling.

'Thank you, please call me Mina.'

After everyone was on board, the vehicle moved away from the landing area and drove a few minutes to a row of small buildings. The group quickly dismounted and entered the nearest building to find a pleasantly air condition de-briefing room, where fresh coffee, water and soft drinks had been laid out for them.

'How was it?' said Mathew to Jack.

'If I had to do it again, I'd pass, mate,' said Jack laughing.

'Specially those bloody camels,' shouted Danny.

Turning back to Jack, Matt said, 'You have the treasure?'

'We sure do. Just a second. Ian, the intel please, buddy.'

Ian came over and handed a light nylon rucksack to Jack, who placed it on the table. Unzipping the bag he said, 'Steve's team found this little lot when they found The Fox. A laptop, three cell-phones, a state of the art satellite-phone and all these ledgers.'

'Excellent,' said Mathew nodding his head, 'excellent work, gentlemen, well done.'

'Your boys back in London should be able to get something worthwhile from all this I hope?' said Tom.

'I'm sure they will and I intend to get this back to London with all haste.'

'I thought you promised us all beers,' said Danny grinning.

'Will you take a rain-check, guys?' said Mathew.

'We're nae takin any kind o' cheque from a spook,' said Ian laughing.

'Her Majesty's Government owes you all a good drink,' said Matt. 'Let's all get together in London as soon as possible. Sorry but I need to go, Jack. There's a cargo plane going back to the UK in the next hour and I need to be on it.'

'No problem, Matt, I understand.'

'Is our ride here?' said Tom.

'Yes, Dimitri's corporate jet has been here for a couple of hours. I guess you can leave as soon as you like.'

'Great. Thanks, Matt, see you in London,' said Tom.

Mathew shook hands with Tom and then hugged Jack. 'See you in London very soon,' then he raised his hand in salute, 'Good bye for now, gentlemen.'

As Matt was leaving, Gareth Mallory and Sergeant Harris entered the briefing room.

'Hello Lieutenant. Didn't expect to see you again,' said Tom.

'No, of course. The thing is, my sergeant here was wondering about your weapons and equipment.'

'Lieutenant, we meet again,' said Jack, 'what can we do for you, sir?'

'Sergeant Harris pointed out to me that you have some very nice American equipment, the Mac10's and a particularly nice sniper rifle; along with some other items that our little squad could use. If you've finished with them of course?'

'We were supposed to return the gear to the Yanks in Erbil,' said Jack, 'but as they failed to pick us up, I guess the gear was all lost. So please help yourself.'

Sergeant Harris smiled and went to the door, 'Okay, lad's, it's your birthday, get this lot into the Landrover.'

The four troopers entered and swiftly collected the weapons and equipment.

'Thank you again, Gareth.' said Jack.

'Have fun with that lot, Sergeant,' said Tom, as he shook the big man's hand.

Chapter Thirty Two
'Two to Erbil'

The big covered truck pulled up to the side of the Orel Corporation jet. When Mina saw the gleaming aircraft she said, 'Is this yours, Jack?'

'My father-in-law's.'

Caroline, one of the corporation's British cabin crew was waiting at the foot of the steps as the dishevelled band approached.

'Good afternoon, gentlemen, madam. Goodness me, we have been in the wars.'

'Hello, Caroline,' said Jack, 'good to see you again. Yes, I'm afraid you'll have to excuse our appearance.'

'I hope you've plenty of beer on board?' said Danny.

'Probably not enough, sir,' she said with a gleaming smile.

Once every one was on board, Jack went along to the flight deck, 'Afternoon, Mike, good to see you again.'

'You too sir, I believe you've had a little trouble?'

'Just a little,' said Jack, grinning, 'What's the flight plan?'

'Straight back to Dubai, sir.'

'Would it be too much trouble to drop a couple of people off in Iraq?'

'Where in Iraq, sir?

'Erbil.'

'No problem, sir. Once we're airborne we'll get clearance from Erbil Air Traffic Control.'

'Thank you, Mike.'

'You're welcome, sir.'

The aircraft took off over the sparkling Mediterranean, climbed to altitude and then banked and turned sharply south-east as it levelled off. The seat belt lights went out and Caroline appeared from the rear of the cabin carrying a silver tray. She went straight to Dan and handed him a tall crystal glass of ice cold lager.

'Orel Airways,' he said, as he raised the glass in mock salute. Then after drinking the contents in one, continued, 'best airline in the world.'

Everyone laughed.

The jet made exceptionally good flying time to Iraq, from wheels up on Cyprus to touch down in Erbil was only an hour and forty minutes. The sleek aircraft was met at the end of the runway by a small truck with an illuminated FOLLOW ME sign on its roof. They came to a stop at the end of the main terminal building and everyone disembarked. Sarmad and Mina were embraced by everyone, with Danny holding on to Mina for a little more than was polite.

'You'll be okay here, doc. Sarmad will look after you and we'll see you in the not too distant future. Thank you for all your help.'

'Goodbye for now, Jack. God bless.'

They all watched in silence as the couple walked away and then waved as they disappeared in to the terminal building.

'Right,' said Ian, 'Orel Island an' a wee bit o' sun, afore I get back tae thet bloody Scottish rain.'

Fifteen minutes later they were in the air heading south-east towards the Persian Gulf and Dimitri's island.

Chapter Thirty Three
'Disavowed'

Tom and Steve had spent a couple of days on the island with the team, then they'd sailed Tom's yacht back up to Dubai. The rest of the guys had stayed on Orel for a few more days and enjoyed the abject luxury of Dimitri's fabulous island. After Jack and Nicole had waved them off from the helipad, Nicole said, Now, Mr Castle I have you all to myself again.'

The following morning Nicole had gone into Dubai shopping with Olga, Dimitri's PA. Jack was on the patio in front of their villa, when his smartphone beeped. He swiped the screen and said, 'Jack Castle.'

'Good morning, Jack, its Mathew.'

'Hi, Matt. How're you doing?'

'I'm fine. How are you feeling now, Jack? Are you getting any rest down there on the island?'

'I'm good, taking it easy now all the lads have gone. Nikki is spoiling me. She's taken some time off work.'

'Nice. Give her my love.'

'Yeah, will do. So what's up Matt?'

'Right. Just thought you might like to know we've had all the ledgers you recovered translated. We had a bit of an issue cracking the laptops' fire-wall because Hamady had a 'Nero Protocol' protecting the hard drive.'

'What the hell is that?'

'Nero. He fiddled while Rome burned.'

'Yes, I do know who Nero was.'

'The protocol, if not disabled would have burned through the hard-drive.'

'Ahh, understood. But you're in now?'

'Our tech guys are milking the info as we speak. But we were surprised to see our old friend Gregg Stoneham's name appear a few times in one of The Fox's ledgers.'

'Really?' said Jack, 'so the bastard is a traitor?'

'A traitor maybe, perhaps a double agent. We've passed some of the intel over to our cousins across the pond in Langley, we'll let them have the treasure from the laptop once we've downloaded it all first of course.'

'Of course,' said Jack laughing.

'The thing is, Jack, they are saying Stoneham was not a double and that he's not been seen or heard from since the Syrian mission.'

'Strange they'd tell you that. They don't usually air their dirty linen in public.'

'Exactly. Very strange,' said Mathew.

'Are they hanging him out to dry? Have they disavowed him?'

'We don't know, Jack.'

'So if the bastard is not a double then he's gone rogue?'

'Precisely, which means he's fair game and we can go after him as well.'

'But won't the CIA want to get to him first?'

'Of course they will. But I'm sure you and your guys would like to catch up with him before they do?'

'We would indeed and I know just how to find him,' said Jack, grinning.

Chapter Thirty Four
'KGB Cocktail'

Nicole and Jack had been back in London for almost four weeks and in that time Dimitri's ex KGB pals hadn't come up with anything about the missing agent. Jack knew it wouldn't be easy to find Gregg Stoneham. He'd operated in the shadowy world of espionage for over thirty years, but by the fifth week Dimitri's old friends had come up with the rogue agent's whereabouts.

Tom had flown up from Dubai and was waiting in the first class lounge at Istanbul's Ataturk Airport. Jack's flight from Heathrow had been delayed and it was almost nine thirty in the evening when he walked into the lounge.

The info they'd been given said that Stoneham was staying at the five-star Magda International Hotel, on the Asian side of the city, overlooking the Straight. They left the terminal and joined the short 'VIP Taxi' queue. The ride from the airport to the hotel although comfortable, took over an hour and a quarter through the busy city and across the Bosphorus Bridge, so it was almost eleven-o-clock when the two friends entered the elegant hotel. Jack scanned the foyer area and quickly saw who he was looking for. 'There he is, Tom. I'll be right back.'

He walked over to the seated man, nodded discreetly, then picked up the large briefcase at the side of the man's chair. Without a word he returned to Tom at the reception desk. Stoneham had checked into the hotel under the name, Robert Jackson and had one of the executive suites on the top floor of the hotel. The receptionist had called the suite, but there'd been no reply, which was exactly what they had hoped for. They took the express lift to the top floor and, at the suite door Jack held the briefcase open as Tom took out the digital key-card bypass. He swiped the card over the small reader screen and the door clicked open.

Once inside the room Jack opened the briefcase again and took out two blue disposable paper coveralls, with attached shoes and hoods and two pairs of latex gloves. They quickly dressed in the comical outfits and as Tom searched the opulent lounge, Jack searched the bedroom and bathroom. Their tasks completed they settled down to wait for Stoneham to return.

It was a little after one in the morning when voices were heard outside the door. Tom and Jack quickly concealed themselves and waited for the agent to enter. The door opened and they heard a woman chattering in broken English and giggling. The door was closed and the lock was heard being slipped. From behind the plush window curtains Jack watched as Stoneham went to the bar; as he bent down Tom was on him. After a vicious blow to the kidneys he deftly slipped a steel wire garrotte over the man's head, pulled it tight around his neck, then dragged the wheezing man from the bar area. The woman screamed as Jack came from behind the curtain.

'Shhhh...' said Jack, raising his hands in a non-threatening gesture, 'it's okay.'

Tom pulled Stoneham to the centre of the room and kept the tension on the garrotte, as the agent clawed at his throat, gasping for breath. Together they flipped him over onto his stomach, Tom knelt on his back as Jack search him for weapons; finding none he quickly recovered the briefcase from behind the couch and removed a roll of duct-tape. After securing the struggling man's wrists and ankles, he reached into his inside pocket and retrieved a wallet. Tom had released the garrotte and the helpless agent groaned and coughed, gulping air into his oxygen starved lungs.

'How much?' Jack asked the woman.

'Five hundred dollars,' she said with a large smile.

Jack removed all the bills from the wallet, quickly did a count and said, 'There's over a grand here. Take it. You were never here. Understand?'

The woman smiled, 'Sure, sure. I never liked him anyway.'

'Bitch,' said Stoneham.

'Shut the fuck up,' said Tom, with a sharp kick to the prone agent's ribs.

Jack unlocked the door and gestured for the woman to leave. As she passed him she stroked his face and said with a smile. 'Sure I can't do anything for you, baby?'

'Not tonight, love. On your way.'

After locking the door, Jack and Tom unceremoniously pulled the man from the floor and threw him on the couch.

'Now then, let's have a little chat,' said Jack.'

'You think you amateurs scare me?' said Stoneham defiantly.

'I'm sure we don't,' said Tom smiling, 'but you're the one bound up and we're here in these silly fucking coveralls.'

Jack noticed the man moving slightly and went to the case again. Taking out two Smith and Wesson revolvers he showed them to Stoneham, 'Don't waste your time trying to recover this from the back of the couch. We found it earlier mate and the other one under the mattress.'

'Smith and Wesson,' said Tom, 'old school spy eh?'

'Fuck you,' snarled the agent.

'Okay, now the pleasantries are over let's move on,' said Jack.

Tom went to the open briefcase and took out a small clear vial of liquid, along with a disposable hypodermic syringe.

'We don't have a lot of time, Gregg. Okay if I call you Gregg?'

'As I just told your sidekick. Fuck you.'

As Tom filled the hypodermic from the vial, Jack continued, 'We aren't in the business of messy torture, waterboarding, or electric shocks. Although Tom is pretty good at pulling out fingernails. We're not even going to chop your balls off. Though we did consider it when you hung us out to dry in Syria. After all, we're British and a little more civilised. So what we're going to do is shoot a little cocktail into you and leave it up to you to decide if you want to talk or not. That okay with you Gregg?'

'What the fuck is that?' snarled Stoneham, 'Scopolamine?'

'It's a little something that a Nazi doctor in the concentration camps was working on. It was very nasty back then. The KGB got hold of the compound and refined it; they even managed to develop an antidote.'

Tom picked up another vial of clear liquid and waved it at the agent.

'But whether we give you the antidote, is entirely up to you, Gregg,' said Jack.

'Go ahead,' smiled Stoneham, 'Scopolamine doesn't scare me.'

'Who said it was Scopolamine?' said Jack, 'it does contain Scopolamine, but with a few other ingredients. Curare, which I'm sure you're familiar with and a little heroin. But the nastiest element comes from a pretty little South American poisonous tree frog.'

Tom approached the couch and instinctively the agent leaned back into the plush cushions.

'The effects are unique, Gregg. The first thing to happen is the heroin kicks in and creates a euphoric state that lasts for about fifteen minutes. Then the other ingredients do their work. They attack the synapses in the brain. You'll feel like your flesh is being burnt off with a blow torch. Your intestines will contract and feel as though they are being drawn from your body. Lastly your heart will be overwhelmed and will be beating so rapidly it will explode and feel as though it has burst out of your chest. '

'Just like the little Alien,' said Tom, with a big grin.

'You'll die in a most unimaginable state of agony,' said Jack, 'unless you get the antidote within twenty minutes, of course.'

Without warning Tom swiftly jabbed the needle into the man's neck. Stoneham did not move for several seconds then his body went into a slight spasm. His face became flushed and his eyes closed as the spasm stopped. He opened his eyes and breathed slowly, then looked at Jack, 'Gimme the antidote. Please, I'll tell you anything you want to know.'

'You'll get that after you tell us everything. Start talking Gregg, you only have twenty minutes, mate.'

Fifteen minutes later, Jack stood up and took out his smartphone, pressed a speed-dial number and said, 'Hi, did you get all that?'

The voice on the other end said, 'Cheers, Jack, we got it all. We'll be right up.'

Tom and Jack took off the disposable coveralls and rolled them up. Tom dropped the garrotte into the briefcase, along with the syringe, vials and latex gloves, their coveralls were last to go in and the case was closed.

'The antidote!' screamed Stoneham, 'you bastards said you'd gimee the antidote.'

'Will you tell him, or shall I?' said Tom, grinning.

'Yeah, you tell him,' said Jack.

'Gregg, my old mate. There is no antidote.

'Oh god, no,' moaned Stoneham.

'Because there is no Nazi, KGB cocktail. I gave you a little shot of adrenalin. That's what brought on the initial euphoria twenty minutes ago. Jack comes up with a scary story and you fell for it. You'll be fine. Well that is until you're back with your pals in Langley.'

Jack went over to the door and unlocked it. A few seconds later Mathew Sterling entered, accompanied by two very fit looking young men, in smart linen suits.

'You remember, Mathew, don't you, Gregg?' said Jack. , 'We're handing you over to MI6, buddy. These gentlemen are going to take you to the British Embassy. You'll stay there until we let your friends in Langley know where you are. My guess is you'll soon be off to the sunny Caribbean.'

'Yeah, for a fucking long time ya' bastard,' said Tom.

'Okay, we're outta here,' said Jack.

Tom, then Jack, shook hands with Mathew. Jack smiled and said, 'See you in London.'

'Yes, see you in London, Jack.'

Four days later, a solemn faced Gregg Stoneham, dressed in a bright orange coverall and accompanied by three CIA operatives, boarded a US government chartered aircraft and took off from the cargo area of Ataturk Airport. The long flight from Turkey to Washington DC was made in silence.

Chapter Thirty Five
'Vauxhall Cross'

Several weeks had passed since he and Tom had extracted the initial information from Stoneham in the Istanbul hotel. Jack had heard the traitor had been moved to some unknown location for further interrogation by his old colleagues from Langley, but all that was behind him now as he worked away in the large garden of their Berkshire home. The day was warm for early May and with his exertions and the thick jumper he wore, Jack had worked up a real sweat. He went back into the kitchen and took a bottle of water from the chiller.

'Lunch in twenty minutes, darling,' said Nicole.

He kissed her and then gulped down the refreshing liquid, spilling some down his chin, as the smartphone beeped; he wiped his mouth on the back of his sleeve, then stroked the screen.

'Jack Castle, good afternoon.'

'Jack, it's Mathew.'

'Matt, how's it going?'

'Good. Are you busy tomorrow for lunch, Jack?'

'Nothing I can't change. Where do you want to eat?'

'Vauxhall Cross Building. Is that okay?'

'Now why would you want to have lunch in the British Secret Service head offices?'

'Don't worry, Jack, it's nothing sinister. Fact is, the balcony restaurant has an excellent chef and the food is first class. Also the Director General wants to meet you.'

'Okay. And why would that be?'

'The treasure you and your guys recovered in Syria has turned out to be golden. Can't discuss over the phone, but I'll give you the bigger picture tomorrow. Can you be here at one o'clock?'

'Sure, why not?'

'I'll meet you at the main entrance and escort you in. See you at one.'

The phone went silent and as Jack walked back out to the big garden he smiled, 'Lunch with the spooks,' he said out loud, 'whatever next?'

'What did you say?' said Nicole.'

'Nothing, babe. Just talking to myself.'

The following day was damp and overcast, with a light drizzle. Jack had driven to the station and travelled into the city by tube, alighting at Vauxhall station, a couple of minutes' walk from the secret service's head office. Although he was almost ten minutes early, Mathew was at the entrance.

'Always early,' said Mathew smiling.

'Yeah, old habits.'

They walked through the foyer and across to the visitors screening area, where Jack emptied his pockets onto a small tray next to a scanning machine. He walked through the machine and picked up his belongings on the other side, then after nodding to the security guard he and Mathew moved across to a small reception desk, where a uniformed lady asked for some form of ID. Jack handed over his driving licence and after signing the visitors book was given a large plastic badge with a bold red V emblazoned across the British royal logo.

'We need to go straight up,' said Matt, 'the Director General has a few things on today, but she said to bring you up as soon as you arrive. The lift is over here.'

'No point in asking what this is all about?' said Jack.

'All in good time,'

They exited the lift and were greeted by a smartly dressed young man wearing a three piece business suit and regimental tie. 'Good afternoon gentlemen,' he said, 'please come this way.' The man knocked twice on the door and waited a few seconds until a voice said 'Come!'

The three men entered the modest office and waited, as the elegantly dressed woman behind the desk finished her telephone call. Then standing, she smiled and said, 'Mr Castle, what a pleasure to meet you at last, we've heard great things about you. Thank you Gareth, that will be all for now.'

The young man left the room without saying a word, as the woman came around the desk with an outstretched hand.

'My pleasure ma'am,' said Jack, with his most charming of smiles.

'Mathew, lovely to see you again. All goes well?'

'Yes ma'am.'

Pointing to a large leather Chesterfield, she said, 'Please, gentlemen, have a seat. Can I get anyone a quick drink? I say quick and I must apologise, as I have to be in Downing Street at two o-clock.'

'Nothing for me, thank you,' said Jack.

'I'm fine, ma'am,' said Mathew.

The director sat down opposite and looked at Jack for several seconds, 'So, Jack, may I call you, Jack? You let yourself be kidnapped by an extremely vicious bunch of terrorists, taken into the heart of Syria and held captive for several days. Your friends then mounted a rescue mission and you captured The Fox into the bargain? Impressive. You are a very courageous individual, Jack.'

'Not really, ma'am. I did what I had to do to protect my family and my friends,'

'Indeed, indeed you did. Courageous nevertheless. And although we lost The Fox, the intelligence you and your men recovered has turned out to be absolute gold. We of course shared that with our cousins across the pond, where I believe a couple of gentlemen over in Langley want to meet you as well; but that's for another day.'

'Your family is well, Jack? Your friends are all good?'

'Yes thank you, ma'am. Everyone is fine.'

'Excellent, excellent, well if you will excuse me, I really do need to get on. Enjoy your lunch and please give some consideration to what Mathew has to say later.'

The three stood and Jack shook hands with the woman, saying 'A pleasure to meet you, ma'am.'

'Yes, thank you, Jack,' she said as she opened the door, 'I'm sure we'll meet again.'

'What the fuck was that all about?' said Jack, quietly, 'How's my family and friends? She doesn't even know them.'

'Small talk, Jack. She just wanted to get a look at you. To weigh you up.'

'Weigh me up? For what?'

The smart dining room was busy and they had to wait a few minutes before being greeted by the restaurant manager.

'Afternoon, Michael,' said Matt, 'I have a table for two booked.'

'Good afternoon, sir,' replied the manager, 'one second please,' then turning to the small reception desk he checked the computer screen and said, 'Yes. If you'll follow me please, gentlemen. It's a little wet today, so we're not using the outside area. I hope you'll be comfortable here.'

'This is perfect. Thank you, Michael.'

'Your waiter will be with you directly, gentlemen. Enjoy your lunch.'

'Okay, what's this all about, Matt?'

'Right, first things first. The treasure you gathered from The Fox has, as the DG said, turned out to be golden. It took us a while to crack the firewall and download all the hard-drive information from his laptop. It was easy enough to translate the notebooks and ledgers, although some of them were in code, but again our guys have cracked that too. Bottom line is we now know what these people are planning.'

'Good. I'm glad it was worth recovering,' said Jack.

'You don't understand. The information we gleaned tells of a ten year planned expansion of ISIL across Syria and Iraq and into other areas of the Middle East. It has cells all over the middle east and down into Africa. These bastards are gonna be more of a problem than Al Qaeda ever was. The ledgers contained information on scores of bank accounts, all over the world, with millions and millions of dollars ready to fund their fanatical regime, but we are going to be able to access most of the accounts and close them down. We're going to develop a specialist counter terrorist group in the heart of the Middle East and attack these guys on their own turf, before they grow.'

'All sounds good,' said Jack, 'but won't you need a full scale boots on the ground coalition to have any real chance of stopping them?'

'Probably yes, but that's gonna be in the future. Right now we can take a covert war to them, thanks to the intelligence you and your guys recovered.'

'Okay, good. Only too pleased to be of assistance,' said Jack, as he raised his glass of water in a mock toast.

'Well, actually, we were hoping you could continue to be of assistance.'

'What now?'

'My boss, Sir Geoffrey Mathers is retiring from the Middle East Desk and I'm being promoted into the position, as Head of Operations.'

'Congratulations, Matt, that's great news. Will you be happy to be stuck in an office though?'

'Oh I think so. There's a lot more to do now and I have some ideas I'd like to implement. The thing is, we'll now need someone to head up the Middle East Station.'

'Right. Who you got in mind?'

Mathew paused for a few seconds and then said, 'You, Jack.'

After lunch Jack left the building and walked along the Albert Embankment. It was raining steadily and he pulled his collar up against the chill afternoon air. He found a sheltered seat on a bench under a large sycamore tree and watched the River Thames roll by for several minutes; then took out his smartphone and pressed a speed-dial number.

'Jack, good to hear from you, mate. What's happening?'

'Hi, Tom. You busy?'

'I'm out on the yacht.'

'Oh, nice.'

'What's up, Jack?'

'How soon can you meet me in Beirut?'

THE END
(For now!)